The Cardinal – Goodnight Kiss for a Child

I0668092

Description

The kiss a mother gives a child before they slip into their dreams, a kiss on the forehead, one on each eye, and one on the lips is a special gift that opens the doorway to that special world.

Elect-Si acquires a daughter and marries Manuel as her existence as Gatekeeper between the spirit world and the physical continues. But now she finds she is also the Gatekeeper of time. The past, the NOW, and the future, she can see the boundary and how unknown the future is and how those who exist in the past cannot be allowed to pass into the NOW, or the future.

Her marriage brings children of her own. Treasured and special in their own way they challenge her to blend all the duties of motherhood, protector of the NOW and the future with her mother's plan to ensure a female vampire continues to sit on the Eastern Papal throne.

The plan is threatened by the appearance of vampire species, unknown until now who can pass on their enzymes, their venom, through ways other than biting with fangs as her mother and she does.

"Did you sleep well?" Asked Elect-Si

Persephone twirled the flower she had picked between her fingers and smelled the beautiful scent. Gently, she moved the petals and looked at the delicate stamen and pistols of the centre of the flower. All around her, bees buzzed excitedly as they scurried from flower to flower harvesting the pollen. As she held the flower, a bee hovered close by it, as if debating whether to land on it and investigate or move on. It decided to move to a flower that had not been picked.

"I was picking flowers in a field when the god Hades saw me. It was such a beautiful day, blue sky, small white clouds like sea foam crossing the great arc of light that is the heavens. The Gods had given me such a wonderful day. I wanted it to go on forever. The field was covered in all kinds of flowers." Persephone paused and looked at more flowers but did not pick any more than the one she held.

"Mother could have sent a slave to pick the flowers to make the villa beautiful but I said I would go."

Persephone looked at Elect-Si.

"The villa, our fields, overlooked the Aegean. The water that day was calm, blue like the sky, a small breeze was coming in off the sea and it made the flowers sway back and forth as it played with them."

Persephone closed her eyes; her face became serene and peaceful as she recalled all she had seen that day.

"There were always fishing boats searching and collecting the bounty of the sea. But that day, there seemed to be more of them, darting back and forth. Bringing their catch to the dock and selling it quickly so they could go out again and catch more. Fishing had been very good for several days. There was always fresh fish, large ones, and octopus, and squid. Poseidon was generous and filled the nets to over flowing." She paused.

"Father out, larger trading vessels with big sails cut into the calm water, leaving a streak of white sea foam behind them as they sailed back and forth with their cargo." She frowned.

"That day there was a fleet of large triremes, war ships, crossing close to shore. I raised my hand to shield my eyes so I could get a better look at them. So big, huge vessels, three banks of oars. I wondered what it must be like to be a man. To be able to travel to new lands on such a magnificent vessel. To have a sword and shield to fight and struggle. To do great deeds, seize treasure; achieve greatness, honour, and glory."

"With my hand shading my eyes, I did not see the god Hades approach on his gold chariot. He had seen me from the Underworld and desired me, though I did not have any desire for him."

Persephone turned to look at Elect-Si.

"You must believe that, and you must believe I was a virgin." There was a firmness to her voice and a muscle twitched in her jaw line as she locked eyes with Elect-Si.

"They tell a tale that he seduced me to go with him into the Underworld. He did not.

Persephone's hands turned to fists, punching at the air in front of her, and the flower she had been admiring dropped to the floor.

'The first I knew I strong hand had me by my long hair and he was pulling me into his chariot. All the time telling me who he was and that he desired me.' Persephone took a step towards Elect-Si.

'He pushed me to the floor and told me that I could not resist a god like him, and besides, Zeus himself had given permission for him to take me. Still, I struggled, but he placed a foot on my stomach and set his three headed dog Cerberus to guard me as he whipped his horses and soon, we were in his realm, the Underworld.'

Persephone stood very still, her eyes closed.

'That place is dark. It is ugly. Everything is to do with death and the souls of the dead, judgment, and punishment. Hades is stern and without mercy in his determination of the fate of even the smallest child, or the oldest of the old.'

Persephone opened her eyes and looked down at her hands and opened her fists. She knelt down to pick up the flower and started looking closely at it again.

'There are no bright colourful flowers like this in the Underworld. But then, you know that, you have been there.'

Slowly, carefully, Persephone placed the flower in her long hair.

'Soon after we arrived at his palace, he had slaves take me to his bed chamber and strip me. He raped me, over and over again, and again. He forced me until he finally fell asleep.' Her hands came and waved in the air at Elect-Si.

'I sat on the edge of the bed, looking at my bruised thighs and put my hand down there and felt the pain in it … where he had forced it in.' Persephone put her hands over her face, and fell silent.

'Then he reached out and took hold of my hair, he threw me down and forced me again and again. Finally, I fell asleep again.'

Persephone looked up at the ceiling and breathed deeply as she seemed to be studying the rich mosaic images of Indian and Himalayan deities.

'When I woke up, the ceiling in the room was a window on the world of man, the world I had been taken from. I could see the field I had been taken from, I could see the ships on the sea, I could see the clouds, I could see my mother Demeter, searching for me. As the days, weeks and months went by I watched her searching for me in parts of the world I did not know existed. She searched to the very end of the world. As I watched it became less and less painful to be forced by Hades.'

Persephone glared at Elect-Si.

'Can you understand that, can you understand how a woman can become insensitive to being raped? Being used like that? Even if it is by a god?'

Elect-Si remained impassive.

'I have been raped when I was young. I was saved, I was saved by my mother as you were saved by yours.'

Persephone became furious swearing and cursing, her hands moving wildly in the air, her body shook and her head rolled back and then to the side.

'Once! You were forced once! I was forced, over and over, every day.' Her mouth contorted and her eyes locked on to Elect-Si.

'I have been raped every day since I was taken.' She beat her chest with her fists.

'Even when I was pregnant with Hades's children, I was raped.' She stepped closer to Elect-Si, her whirling hands touching Elect-Si.

'He watched as I delivered my first, Melinoe. As she lay in the hands of the midwife, he watched as the cord was cut and he took me by the shoulder and pushed me towards the bedroom to use me, the remains of my daughter's cord hanging between my legs.' Persephone's hands whirled above her head.

'The afterbirth came out on the floor as he pushed me to the bed. Then he was in me.'

Persephone breathed heavily and slowly her arms came to hang limply beside her.

'It is no wonder my precious daughter Melinoe is the Goddess who brings Nightmares and Madness.'

Carefully Persephone adjusted her toga and her breathing slowed and the raging colour in her cheeks grew paler and her face returned to the sweet precious tanned olive colour.

Elect-Si moved around Persephone who for the moment, seemed to be quiet, a spent force, though Elect-Si did not believe that.

'Zeus agreed you should be freed from Hades, but you ate seeds from a pomegranate, fruit that had grown in the Underworld. That bound you to Hades and the Underworld. When Hermes arrived to retrieve you, your taste of those seeds obliged you to spend a third of each year, the winter months to the world of man, in the place that bears his name, Hades. The remainder of the year you spend with the pantheon of Greek Gods, and the physical world of man. You are after all the Goddess of vegetation and grain, the things that bring sustenance to mankind and his animals.'

Abruptly Persephone spun around, her hand reaching out as if to touch Elect-Si's heart. Abruptly Persephone pulled her hand back and she took several steps backward. A mixture of terror, pain, and fear written on her face.

'Such power … even Zeus … it hurts my eyes to look at your heart.' She placed her hands over her heart and turned away.

'So much pain…'

Elect-Si moved around to face Persephone, but as she did, Persephone took a step backwards.

'You must tell me what you want. I cannot judge you without knowing what you desire.'

'You know!' Exclaimed Persephone.

'It is to be free of the Underworld. You have been to the Underworld; you know what it is like there… You visited without permission of Hades.' She breathed slowly but heavily, as if she were building her energy for another outpouring of emotion.

'The tower of light; it was everywhere, even Hades's bed chamber. He was furious that such light should exist in his domain.'

Elect-Si shrugged.

'I do not need his permission. Do you … does he understand that?'

Persephone started to turn away again, but Elect-Si moved so that the two were always facing each other.

'I am a white shaman. I am Gate Keeper between the spirit world, and this one. I go where I please, when I please, and I do what I want there.'

Persephone tried to back away, a small hesitating step at first and then a larger one. Elect-Si mirrored the steps, always making sure the distance between them never changed.

Suddenly, Persephone's eyes flared and her lips contorted in anger.

'I am Goddess of the Underworld. He is God of the Underworld. We cannot allow this!' She lunged forward, one hand drifting towards Elect-Si's heart again, the other, fingers curled into a claw towards Elect-Si's face.

Elect-Si knocked the clawed hand to one side, and with the heel of her other hand she drove it upwards into the jaw of Persephone.

Goddess Persephone's head jerked violently backwards, she grunted as air was expelled from her lungs. The motion brought her other hand closer to Elect-Si's toli. There was a flash of intense, bright, white light, so bright it seemed to remove all colour from furnishings and flowers on the verandah, everything became a pale grey outline for the moment it existed. She screamed in agony and staggered backwards, trying not to fall, whimpering, and clutching her hand close to her chest all at the same time.

Her legs knocked into a chair and she fell into it, making it skid backwards on the floor. She curled forward shielding her injured hand, not daring to look at it.

Elect-Si did not move, she could not see what happened to Persephone's hand but from the sound of the whimpering and crying, she figured it could not be good.

'Get back to the Underworld, go now while I am patient with you. I will not change the agreement you have with Zeus, or the god Hades.'

'You would send me back to be raped, over and over for those months.' Persephone sobbed.

'You are a woman; you know what it is like to be forced. You know how it feels. You are a woman, like me. You would send me back to endure that?'

'Yes!' Abruptly, Elect-Si moved towards Persephone who pushed backwards with her feet moving the chair and giving her space to stand and move away from Elect-Si.

'So cruel, so very cruel.'

'That is the blackness in me.' Elect-Si took a step forward. As she did a breeze ruffled the flowers on the verandah railing.

'I will tell my father, Zeus of this encounter. Of your callous decision against his daughter.'

'It was your father who gave you to Hades, he allowed Hades to come through from the Underworld and take you away to rape and imprison you. Zeus! He fathered one of your children. A daughter having a child by her father, even humans have laws against that. Maybe the Underworld is where you deserve to be.' Elect-Si's eyes narrowed.

'Winter on the Aegean coast is starting, get back to the Underworld, now!'

Cradling her hand, Persephone started to fade and become translucent. The flower in her hair hovered for a moment in the air and then fell to the floor. Persephone looked at the flower on the floor and as she became less and less in this world, she slowly bent down and reached for the colourful bloom. Her hand passed through the flower as it lay on the floor, like the hand of a ghost. Then, she was gone.

Elect-Si moved to straighten the chair and return it to where it had been, as she did, out of the corner of her eye she saw Brielle standing in the open doorway.

'So, that is how it is done?' asked Brielle as she came fully into the room.

Elect-Si adjusted the chair to its final place and stood up turning to face her daughter as she did.

'Yes.'

'Yes!' The word was repeated from behind Elect-Si. Amunet stepped from beside the flowers and walked over to the chair and sat in it.

'Your first hard decision. Sending a woman back to a man, even if he is a god, who will force himself on her every day of the next three months.' Amunet reached under the chin of her fire dragon and stroked it which seemed to make the dragon go to sleep."

"You sound like my guide."

Amunet looked past Elect-Si, to the stone railing of the verandah.

"We were watching, we talked."

Elect-Si turned to look at her guide who as sitting on the railing wall, kicking his feet. He looked at her matter-of-factly.

"Some would say what you did was cruel and heartless. But you did what was right, it was the darkness in you that allowed you to make that decision. You sense it, you know it is there, you do not fear it. You use it." He jumped down from the railing and walked over.

"You know how to manage your blackness very, very well."

"How can Amunet be the Goddess who welcomes souls into the afterlife when Persephone and Hades are Gods of the same thing?" Asked, Brielle.

Elect-Si's guide gestured to Amunet.

"When you look at existence; through Egyptian lens, you see everything Egyptian. When you look through a Greek lens, you see everything Greek."

"And when I go to the Underworld?" Asked Elect-Si

"You see it as it is. You could also step into any belief system you want to. You are not restricted to any religious or spiritual system."

Elect-Si stood quietly for a moment.

"Was it really as bad as it sounds? To send Persephone back?"

"Consequences. You made a decision based on consequences not the spirit who was asking." Amunet looked up as she folded her legs under her.

"Hades would have been next, Demeter to be with her daughter, then Zeus, because you had meddled in his godly decision. In the end, the entire Pantheon of Greek Gods would have emerged into this world. They would have had all their power. Made the same demands of humanity. Humanity would have been left cowering just as they once did."

"Amunet, in the Underworld, you could have let me see it through Egyptian eyes but you did not, you let me see it as it was." Elect-Si was fascinated by the thought of seeing the Underworld through a different lens.

Amunet looked at Elect-Si's guide and then back to Elect-Si.

"I could have, but that is not who I am. We have known each other for so many, many centuries, to make you see the Underworld through my Egyptian eyes would not have been honest with you. Besides, I have moved on from those times. I am more than just the keeper of souls today."

Elect-Si turned to her guide.

"What do you mean you and Amunet have been talking?"

Her guide met her challenging stare.

"There are guides that will come forward to help you with different challenges and learning. Amunet is one of us and she is very unique. She has been with you since your human birth." He paused.

"I know, I know, your mother has known her for millennia as well but you only became aware Amunet as someone you could interact with when you became Lady Challis's daughter."

Elect-Si turned to look at Amunet.

"You mean so much to my mother."

"She is a guide to your mother as well, I said she is unique, it goes further than the meaning of the word. Amunet has always been able to freely move between the spirit world and this one. At first, I did not recognize her for who she is."

"Is that what you meant when I judged her and you said she is blessed?"

"Yes."

Lady Challis looked down from the large open window at the lush, rich gardens of the sanatorium.

Secluded.

Private.

Lavish.

Palatial.

Guarded.

This was a place where those of her kind who needed help came. It was a testament to the resilience of her kind that today, it housed very few.

Her eyes focused on the wispy hair of an old man sitting in a comfortable powered wheelchair. Two nurses with a third supervising a food cart was preparing a meal for him under the branches of a spacious old willow tree. She turned her attention back to the room and the group of doctors. She handed her tablet to Brielle.

"So, we have repaired his body but not his mind?" She said to the leading doctors.

One stood slightly forward from the rest and nodded.

"We have tried all the available treatments and the special ones you suggested. It is centuries since you rescued him, but mentally, he is the same age as the child when you saved him. For many, many decades he read a lot, as if he were studying. He would not say what for, or why. He is stable now but is not improving. Everything is compounded by the drugs the Nazi's administered in an attempt to force his body to create large quantities of his enzymes."

"He should not be as aged as he appears, is that as a result of the drugs?"

"They were milking him sexually as well. Forcing him to produce large quantities of semen. They were trying to find a way to breed vampires using human female prisoners." The doctor paused.

"The horrors he witnessed there, the experiments on humans… A child should not witness those kinds of things. Not even a vampire"

The cocktail of drugs used sped up his metabolism, advanced his aging." The doctor turned his gaze to Brielle who stood reading from the tablet, and then back to Lady Challis.

"He wants to die. He wants an end. He wants it now." Said Brielle looking up from the tablet.

"But he will not do it himself."

The doctor's gaze jerked back to Brielle.

"That is correct. We make sure he always has three attendants with him at all times, just in case he tries to end himself. But death, a vampire's death, he wants it more than anything. '

"It goes against everything we hold dear, to kill another vampire.' Mused Lady Challis as she turned back to the open window.

"His death must not be in vain; it must not go to waste. Said, Brielle.

Lady Challis turned to look at Brielle.

"An autopsy?"

"Yes"

"You know that is desecration of a vampire's body. Our holiest book of death rites specifically forbids it." Lady Challis's stare was direct and unwavering.

"Yes. I do. But I am not of your kind, and neither is Sophyra or Phaedra. They would not waste a moment considering ceremonies and prohibitions for the dead. We need whatever information we can learn." Brielle turned off the tablet and held it to her chest, like a school girl holding a text book.

"I will not breach our traditions, not break our rites." Said the doctor.

Lady Challis turned her attention back to the man in the wheelchair. His meal was ending, the nurses were packing away the food cart. Three new nurses waited for the meal cart to leave before setting up folding chairs, one had a book and some papers with her, they were preparing to spend the afternoon with their patient.

"You will do what you are told," said Lady Challis abruptly. As she turned back to face the doctor.

"Brielle will supervise." She looked at the doctor sternly and then scanned the rest of the medical team.

"Remember. In this matter, when Brielle speaks, she speaks for me. Challenge her, and you challenge me. Is that clear?" Lady Challis waited. No one spoke. All were frozen where they stood.

"We should visit our patient now." She said turning to Brielle.

Lady Challis hugged the old man in the wheelchair, she straightened his hair and kissed his cheek.

"Challis, is it is so good to see you. It has been too long." The voice was thin, wispy, but unwavering. His eyes were warm, deep brown and glittered in the sun light that came through the weeping branches of the Willow Tree.

"You must have received my message?"

"I had expected to see doing better, young, vigorous, and at least chasing the nurses, or, better, out in the world."

"Maybe in the first few years," he rolled up his sleeves and showed his scrawny arms. He ran his hands over them.

"Now look at me, not much left."

He rested his arms on the arm rests of his chair and turned to look at Brielle.

"You are not like Challis or myself. Not like any of us here. I can sense it, you know that?" he waited for a moment before continuing.

"You are here to help me sleep the eternal sleep! I had never expected someone so young. Beautiful."

He looked to Lady Challis and back to Brielle.

"It was a friend of mine who gave me up to the Nazi's." The old man scowled at the memory.

"He could spit his enzymes. He used to enjoy teasing me at how far he could spit saying he was superior to me; he could kill at 10 feet if he needed to. I would have to be close enough to bite and that made me less of a vampire in his eyes, in his parents' eyes."

He looked at Brielle again.

"But you are not like him, you are different again. I knew there were more species of vampire. We and the spitters cannot be alone." He paused.

"We are not alone, are we. You are not the same as Challis and me, or the spitter that betrayed me."

The old Man straightened his shirt and pursed his lips.

"I dreamt about all of this one night, a few days after I arrived. But the dream faded, and none like it appeared again until last night after they told me you were coming to visit me, to see how I am doing. Your message said there was something from the long ago past that you need to ask me about. They said you would not be alone." He looked deeply into Brielle's eyes.

"So long as Challis trusts you, I trust you to do what you are here for."

Brielle picked up one of the chairs and moved it closer to the old man, and sat down.

"I am Brielle. No, I am not the same as Challis or anyone here. I am not the same as those who spit. I am from another, a different species of Vampire." Brielle paused.

"Tell me. What was in the dream?"

The old man rested his head against the pillow on his head rest, a pleasant breeze blew across the garden and ruffled the low-hanging branches. He closed his eyes as he started to speak about his dream.

"I was on a never-ending plain of green grass. I could see animals grazing, a few horses, and deer. The sky was clear and very blue. A few white clouds scurried across it. There was a range of tall mountains close by. One, a pyramid-shaped peak with an overhang that looked like the beak of a great eagle. My feet were in a stream that ran down from the mountains. The stream was unusually strong and fast flowing for its size." He reached for a bottle of water and slowly took a sip.

"I heard a voice from that beautiful sky saying it was he, Tengri, the god of the sky whom the Mongols worshiped." He opened his eyes to look at Lady Challis.

"You know where that stream is, don't you?" He did not wait for an answer, he continued on.

"The water seemed to be speaking to me. Telling me that what I had in my mouth, my fangs that delivered the enzymes of a vampire were not all there is. There were other ways to get the venom into the blood of a victim, or, a lover." He opened his eyes and used the hand control of his chair to turn so that he fully faced Brielle.

"You are one of the other kinds of vampire I was about."

"I do not have fangs. None of my kind has. We scratch and our enzymes come through our nails." Said, Brielle.

He nodded slowly.

"But there is more. There is one other kind." He looked at Lady Challis who was drawing closer. She sat down in a chair. The words were like a magnet. He had her full attention.

"Just as we bite, you scratch, and spitters, spit. There is a kind that can pass their enzymes through touch. If they desire to. It could be a handshake, a clammy handshake. A kiss, a tongue passing across another. Sex … of course, sex, penetration. However, their fluids mix with their victim. They can turn their bodily fluids, like water in a stream into something potent and deadly."

He looked at Brielle.

"When it is time for me to sleep, do as my mother did. Please do not make it painful. I have had enough pain in this life. So much of it while I was with the Nazi's."

Brielle studied his gaze.

"When you go to sleep, it will be as when your mother tucked you in. It will be painless. I promise." She waited. She knew he would say more.

"Do what you have to, after I go to sleep, learn what you can from this brutalized old body."

"Thank you."

The old man looked over at Lady Challis.

"Is there anything else? If not, I would like to sleep now."

Lady Challis sat staring, frozen at the words that had passed between the old man and Brielle. She felt a lump in her throat.

"There is nothing else." She stammered. Her hand covered her mouth in case her lips betrayed her feelings.

He turned and looked at Brielle, and smiled.

"Now would be a good time mother."

Brielle stood up and rested her hand on the thin wrist closest to her. She leaned forward, whispering so that even Lady Challis had to strain to hear,

"My beautiful son, you lived a life that should not have been lived by you. A life I did not want for you. A life I did not carry you for so long and then to have you endure such pain." She leaned further forward and kissed the old man on the forehead. Stroking his thin hair as a mother might stroke the hair of her child going to sleep. She moved her lips down to his now-closed eyes and kissed each tenderly in turn. Finally, she kissed his lips.

"A Goodnight Kiss for a child…" Said Brielle softly.

The old man smiled, but did not open his eyes.

"Thank you, Mother, for all you have done for me, and, for what you are about to do."

Brielle tightened her grip on his wrist and rested her other hand on his forearm. Suddenly, her hand took the form of a claw and her nails dug in. She pulled down and left four, short, scratch marks.

The old man sat still for a moment as if listening to the birds in the Willow Tree. Then, slowly as if he were going to have a nap, his head rolled forward and his chin rested on his chest.

All around there was silence. No birds sang and no breeze ruffled the tree, or the grass, or the flowers. There was nothing. Brielle stood up and let go of the old man's wrist, placing his hand on his lap. Gently, she rested the other hand on top. She turned to look at Lady Challis who was frozen, and speechless.

"How did you know?" Asked Lady Challis.

"The kiss? That is how my mother, Ximena, kissed me. She would tuck me in, and after telling me a story. She straightened my hair and kissed me that way. I always went to sleep after she kissed me that way." She looked down at the old man.

"We are different but the same in so many ways."

Lady Challis's eyes focused on the short, maybe half inch scratches.

"That is all it takes?"

Brielle looked down, somewhat surprised at the short length and depth of the scratches.

"He was already dying, not much of my enzyme was required." She turned to look at Lady Challis.

"But I have never killed a fanged vampire before. I did my best to make it fast and painless."

"You did very well. It was completely painless, his soul thanks you." The voice was clear and crisp, but very gentle.

Brielle turned fully around.

"Thank you, Amunet."

Lady Challis looked in the direction Brielle was staring, an unspoken question on her face.

"I have his soul. It will be lovingly cared for." Amunet was now close to Brielle and Lady Challis. She reached out and held Brielle's arm.

"He says it was fast and painless, he cannot stop thanking you… He loves you for what you did." She paused and rubbed Brielle's arm.

"You may not need a full autopsy, look at the Pineal and Pituitary glands. They are different in vampires from humans. Fangs, spitting, scratching and touch, they are just delivery mechanisms, adaptations to the needs of a vampire's environment."

"That is from him?"

"Yes. He said his understanding came from reading and studying evolution, and his own body when he first arrived." Said Amunet.

"Tell him, thank you." Said, Brielle.

Amunet drew closer to Brielle.

"I am letting him see and hear through my eyes and ears. He knows." She moved closer still and kissed Brielle on the cheek.

"That is from him."

Lady Challis fluttered her wings before folding them away. She stood on the bank of a fast-flowing stream, it moved quickly and silkily across the rocks at its bottom and under the overhanging bank on the other side. Lady Challis turned to look at the tall mountain range to her right.

A pyramid like mountain could be clearly seen and the eagle's beak created by overhanging rock stood out black and pointed.

"We are near the Tian Shan mountain range close to the Chinese border. I am not sure if we are in Kazakhstan or Kyrgyzstan." Lady Challis reflected on the last time she had been here. No borders, no countries except for China which had already been conquered by the Great Lord Chinggis. She could ride where she wanted, when she wanted, and so did her men. She turned away from the mountains and looked over the beginning of the rolling grasslands of the Mongolian Plateau.

A herd of deer were coming over the top of a ridge and stood for a moment taking in the green grass and blue sky. They looked around at the feast that lay before them. Some chose to move down the slope to feed, some stayed where they had stopped and ate there.

"This is so amazing," Brielle said from behind her.

"The grass is never ending, the sky is never ending, the peace and quiet. But you know, I have a feeling that if this Tengri, God of the sky wanted to extend a finger, he could squash us out of existence so easily." She sat down on a convenient large boulder that seemed to have been washed down from the mountains close by.

Away downstream there was splashing and a large sigh. Amunet was swimming, it seemed as though the water temperature was quite acceptable for such sport, but Lady Challis highly doubted it. They were too close to the mountains and the melting snow for it to be anything other than freezing.

Lady Challis turned to Brielle.

"Thoughts … your thoughts on the results from studying the Pineal and Pituitary glands."

Brielle picked a long blade of grass and started to eat it.

"Enzymes are a cocktail of natural chemicals in the body. If they weren't, the body receiving it would reject it. The glands are responsible for balancing the enzyme mix according to the vampire's purpose."

"So, when the old man went to sleep, you balanced the enzyme mix so he would die a swift, painless death?"

"Here's the thing. I knew what I wanted to happen, what I intended to happen, but nothing I am aware of came up with a recipe for the correct mix of enzymes. Unconsciously, I knew what was required." Brielle looked at Amunet who was walking towards them, ringing water from her long black hair. Overhead, her fire dragon made playful circles in the still air.

"Isn't the water cold? Its snow melt from the mountains."

Amunet smiled.

"Not for me, it is like the Nile in winter. Try it!"

Lady Challis suddenly struck by a question of why they were there, walked towards the bank and sat down, kicking off her shoes, and fearing the cold temperature of the stream she gingerly put her feet into it. She was surprised to find the temperature quite pleasant, not warm, just pleasant.

Instinctively, she looked up at the blue sky and gave thanks Tengri. As she looked down at the grass her hands were resting on, she felt surprise at how easy it had been to look up and thank Tengri just as she had so often done when she was part of the Mongol empire. She could almost feel the cool wind from the snow-covered mountains on the back of her neck. She had brought her army through the winding mountain passes, avoiding those more treacherous and deadly.

She had flown through the mountain passes many times but no one knew. Her ability to bring her army through to the green pastures and blue sky depended on that secret knowledge gleaned from Mother Earth as a vampire. It served to deepen the veneration her men held for her.

"Don't lose yourself in the past." The voice was close by, she looked up to see Brielle kneeling beside her.

"You need to be in the Now. With us."

"How did you know?" Whispered Lady Challis as she looked into Brielle's eyes.

"A guess, the expression on your face. I have done the same … lost myself in the past."

"But you are so young, sorry, I did not mean it that way."

Brielle looked at the mountains for a moment, then down at the stream and then back into Lady Challis's eyes.

"There is so much more that makes my kind different from you. It is more than the finger nails. You live and experience life and carry memories of experiences forward. Maybe that is because you are immortal. My kind accumulates and carries forward memories from each existence to the next. No one knows how we do it. But I have the memories of everyone in my linage. You may see me as a teenager, but if you could look inside, you would see someone as old as you."

Lady Challis studied the young, mature face.

"That is what has made you immortal, all the memories, the heritage?"

"Yes. If I were not immortal, my death would result in the loss of so much heritage. I guess it has one benefit, I do not have to live and experience all the lives of which I have memories."

"What about your mother, Ximena?"

"I have her memories, up to the moment of her death."

"She was obviously not immortal?"

"Her role was to pass on the memories she had accumulated to me. I was to be immortal. There is always a point in existence when the chain can be broken, heritage lost by the death of one who is not immortal. But I was born before her death so I had all the memories she had, all I had to live and experience was her life." Brielle sighed; she ran her fingers through the grass. As if making a decision, she turned towards Lady Challis.

"I have never told anyone this." She paused.

"The stories she told me each night were not fairy tales. Oh no! They were memories from the past, often, the dim and very distant past. They were a test. I was to use my copy of the memory to interpret and correct her. Each night she tested me, a different memory, a different age, a different experience."

"So, the goodnight kiss you gave the old man … you saw it from the view point of your mother's memories, and from your own experience?"

"Yes, exactly." Smiled, Brielle.

Elect-Si cleaned Canasta's chin and leaned over the edge of the baby's bed to lay her down. Just before her little bum hit the mattress, arms and small fists started assailing her forearms and hands, feet started kicking as if the baby were doing some outrageous martial art.

Abruptly she stopped putting Canasta down and instead picked her up and held her to her chest. Elect-Si's eyes opened at the indignant words Canasta was speaking.

"No! No! No more milk, my belly is still small. I have had enough! What did I tell you yesterday, don't lay me down on my back? The ceiling is beautiful, but I have been lying on my back staring at it for a month now. It is fracking boring. Go down by the reflecting lake, and take me with you!"

Holding Canasta close and supporting her head so she could look at her in the eyes, Elect-Si thought.

"Don't swear!"

Canasta was still for a moment and then closed her eyes, her small mouth opened and her chest seemed to expand. She scrunched up her small face and her body seemed to shake. All of a sudden, she sneezed violently. Her top lip, mouth, and chin were covered with snot. Clean that up!" A small voice demanded.

"Challis, you look so tired … are you alright?" Elect-Si rested her hand on the back of her mother's neck. She could feel the tension and the tiredness.

Lady Challis pulled her cup of coffee closer to her lips so she could smell the elixir.

"Can you imagine how fast Brielle flies? No, I guess you can't you haven't flown with her over really long distances." Lady Challis looked across the breakfast table at Amunet.

"If it had not been for you, I would have never seen her circling in the sun, waiting for me."

Amunet leaned forward and sipped at her child water.

"She has memories from all the past lives in her lineage. They came from the deep deserts of Afrika. They learned how to use the thermals, flying from one to another." She hesitated as she looked at Lady Challis.

"Much better than you…" She shrugged.

"Just saying … also, she is a predator. You can spot prey much easier from high up when hidden by the sun. At that height, you can decide how to kill it before you have committed to an attack. Also, her wings are very pale-coloured, and blend in well with the sky when you look up."

"Brielle, is a predator?"

"Oh yes! She is a weapon, use her against Sophyra and Phaedra."

"I have flown with her to the Himalayas. I thought I was slow because I was pregnant. She always waited for me." Interrupted Elect-Si.

"I guess you are talking about me, my ears are burning!" Brielle sat down beside Lady Challis.

"I did not mean to challenge your flying if that's what you are discussing."

Lady Challis held out her coffee mug to get it refilled.

"To be honest, I have never flown so far, so fast, even with Amunet's help."

Leaning across the table, Brielle looked at Amunet.

"Thank you so much! I have never experienced thermals and wind channels like the ones you provided."

"You are very welcome." Smiled Amunet.

Brielle looked around the table.

"I have results. Is everyone ready?" She did no wait, she turned on her tablet.

"Fanged vampires are quite easy, no offence intended. Because you bit through the surface skin layer and inject directly into the victim's blood, your enzymes have virtually no obstacle to overcome and mix directly into the blood. Whether you want to kill, retain the victim for future feeding, or turn them into another vampire, that comes down to intent and that influences the composition of the venom."

She looked around the table. No one said anything.

"Spitters such as Sophyra. The venom has to be thick enough that it can be balled in the throat before a strong blast of air from the lungs pushes it out. It has to retain the ball shape in the air. When it hits a surface, the ball breaks and if it is skin, it has to stick to it until it is absorbed through the skin. The rest is the same." Brielle looked around the table.

She wiggled her fingers in the air.

"Scratchers, like Phaedra and myself. If we scratch deeply enough, we can break the surface layer of the skin, including the layer of dead skin. Our venom is designed to be absorbed very, very quickly and behaves the same as fanged vampires. If we have direct access to the blood stream, through a wound for example, our venom behaves the same as fanged vampires."

Lady Challis moved awkwardly in her chair. The tension in her sore back and wing muscles was making sitting painful.

"Sophyra seems to have the most issues to overcome. Fangs and nails break the skin allowing the enzymes access to the blood stream quickly."

"Fangs and scratchers. We can get the enzymes into the victim's blood in two, maybe, three seconds and whatever we intend for the victim, is complete in 5 or 6." Brielle waited but again seeing no reaction continued.

"Venom from a spitter will take as much as 10 seconds, or even longer to be absorbed, then it starts work in 6 to 8 seconds. Here is the kicker. To spit any distance, a larger ball of enzymes has to be produced to give it enough mass to travel more than just a few feet."

Elect-Si's eyes locked on to Brielle's "Sophyra is at a disadvantage, all spitters are at a disadvantage."

"There is more. You and I can change the intent of our enzyme mix virtually at the moment we break the skin. Sophyra cannot, the moment the ball is created and stabilized for spitting she is locked into the results of her intention at that moment. Rather like a human when they aim a gun, and pull the trigger. They can't do anything about the bullet. We can change the bullet until it leaves the muzzle."

Brielle picked up the coffee cup placed in front of her and slowly dunked a short bread cookie in it.

"There is more?" said Elect-Si slowly.

Brielle shook her shoulders and continued eating coffee-soaked cookies. Amunet leaned forward.

"Now is the time."

"Si, I told you one time I could kill Phaedra, that is true." She smiled.

"I am toxic to her. Rather, branch of the species is toxic to her. Also, to Sophyra. I am not toxic to a fanged vampire; you are not toxic to me."

Elect-Si looked at Amunet.

"You knew about this?

Amunet sipped at her water again, slowly she set down her glass and looked at Elect-Si.

'Remember, I receive the souls of the dead, it is not my role to judge, it is not my role to investigate the "how" of death, just the soul. Until Brielle started her report, I had never considered it.' She twirled her glass on the table top.

"There is more … isn't there?" She said looking up at Brielle.

Brielle turned her tablet off. She pressed the tips of her fingers into the sugar and cookie crumbs on her plate and licked them off.

"It seems that fanged vampires, and my strain of Afrikan scratchers can heal each other if we allow the other to inject their enzymes." She looked up.

"Just the species around this table. Phaedra and her variant, they are excluded. Spitters, nothing can be done for them, and we should not allow their venom to land on us. We will not die, but the pain will be disabling. But it will pass."
Lady Challis stared straight ahead, her stare was fixed and unflinching.

"Heal each other?" She set down her mug and turned to Brielle.

"But aren't you also a predator?"

A smile flashed briefly on Brielle's lips.

"Yes, I am a predator, just as you are, as Si is. You do not think of yourself as such, you look outward, and point to other variants and label them as predators or not. If I am not a predator, then I am submissive, a victim." Brielle pushed the now clean plate to one side for a servant to collect.

"A vampire can never be anything other than a predator." She rapped on the table top with the hand for emphasis.

Lady Challis went back to staring straight ahead, listening to a breeze moving the large canopy over the table, pressing on joints and guy ropes, making them creak as the strain changed here and there. Out of the corner of her eye she could see Amunet, sip water and sit back watching her intently. The moments of her decision-making seemed like drips of blood from a goat that had just been killed. Watched over by Lucy, every drip was counted into the gourd beneath the open neck.

She turned to Brielle.

"OK. Now, it would be good."

Brielle looked down at the table cloth and flexed her fingers. She looked up at Elect-Si who was suddenly alert and intent, her hand was reaching for her cane. Her mouth about to open in protest. Amunet was nodding and her fire Dragon was now alert and standing on her shoulder, watching everyone around the table. As she turned back to Lady Challis, she could see a hand go up, cutting off any protest from Elect-Si.

Slowly, Brielle stood up and moved behind Lady Challis. She stroked the long black hair and started to move it to one side to show the back of Lady Challis's neck and the tired, tense neck, back and flight muscles. But as she moved the hair to one side, she allowed herself to scratch Lady Challis's shoulder.

Lady Challis' started to raise a hand to the spot where she had been scratched but then it relaxed on to the arm rest. Her eyes closed and her breathing became quick and short. From somewhere deep inside, she groaned.

Like water from a warm relaxing bath when the plug is pulled, pain, tension, and tiredness drained away.

"Oh! That is so, so very good!"

Brielle's heart sank. Sophyra and Phaedra were going right to the last vampire, a man in his twenties, naked and shackled to the cold stone seminary wall behind him. A ball gag in his mouth to suppress any screams. A painful black stain on his chest. The skin glistened and looked bubbly, and broken at the same time. At the edges, blood oozed out, and dripped on to the floor.

Sophyra world, her arms flashing out from her body, her eyes viciously flaring and her mouth open wide as if she were about cough out a chicken bone. The light from the large window glistened off the ball of venom as it shot through the air like a slow-moving shot gun slug.

The ball of liquid hit the man just below his navel. The skin immediately turned black and started to bubble as if acid had been dropped on to it. He tried to bend over, but his shackles stopped him and held him back. His knees collapsed and he fell back against the wall, staring down at the new centre of pain. His head rolled back and he screamed hopelessly into the gag in his mouth. Underneath him, his legs thrashed wildly.

"Well. That was predictable!" Exclaimed Brielle as she moved forward her hand passing under her leather jacket and slipping the dagger out from the sheath across her lower back. She took hold of the young man's hair and jerked his head back. The eyes looked up at her imploringly, they asked her … yes, now, do it now. Be kind … one moment of kindness … please!

Brielle slipped her blade into that soft space under the chin and up into his brain. The eyes flickered for a moment with thankfulness, gratitude, and then closed.

Brielle wiped the blade and slipped it back into its sheath, as she did, she looked at Pope Sophyra and Phaedra. Who eyed her doubtfully? She turned away from them and slowly walked down the line of bodies still shackled to the wall where they fell. Some with blackened acid stains on their bodies, some with scratches. Others with what appeared to be deep powerful cuts, but clearly made by finger nails.

The testing, if that is what it was, had been going on for days before she got here. She could tell by the dried feces and urine stains by the bodies at the far end. Vampires are just the same as humans in that regard. When the soul passes over and the body stops. The sphincters that control bodily fluids let go and out comes whatever remains inside.

Brielle came to the end of the line, the first vampire to die. Her eyes took in the scene in front of her. A young man, his lips blackened by death and the skin around the teeth starting to pull back. Eye sockets starting to skink into his skull. The shoulders and chest were covered in scratch marks, the deepest in the middle of his chest looked as if they had been made by a small knife.

Next to his penis, the dried white stain of an ejaculation and a small pool of dried white semen. Brielle heard Phaedra come up beside her.

"Where you were doing him when you scratched him."

"Of course! That is what the murder scene tells you, doesn't it?"

Brielle looked at Phaedra, she was smiling and holding her hands together in front of her as if she were going to prey.

"He was a good ride, look at the way he is hung. I got off just before he ejaculated. I wasn't going to let any disgusting spitter come in me." She held up her thumbs and pointed with them at the wound in his chest.

"I came just as his cock dropped out, that is why those scratches are so deep." She said sighing.

"I wanted to see what it was like having one of them," she said, half turning to Pope Sophyra who was standing a few feet away, listening.

"I enjoy screwing and scratching a human I have turned. Cassius, I really enjoyed him but scratching one of them," she pointed to the body.

"It is not the same…" She turned to look at Pope Sophyra as she spoke the last words.

"Oh, don't get all pouty, I let you watch. Watch everything, from start to finish. Maybe you will get more joy out of Father Ambrose now."

"What happens next?" asked Brielle eyeing the line of contorted bodies.

"As soon as I give the word, we will burn the bodies. We have what we need."

"What do you have?" Challenged Brielle.

Phaedra frowned and started to move back to the centre of the room, over her shoulder her slightly raised voice gave her summary.

"Sophyra's kind can kill mine but it takes more than one shot. If you had not stepped in and killed that last experiment, I am sure it would have been another two spits. I can kill a spitter more easily, but of course, I need to get closer." She pointed to two bodies next to each other.

"We even tried killing our own kind with our venom. That didn't work. No effect. We each had to kill the other's kind."

Brielle stared at the bodies with livid scratches and blackened, burnt skin. After a moment she turned away casually so as not to give the information any apparent importance.

Phaedra looked along the line of corpses.

"Brielle, you are a scratcher like me. There are a few extra spitters we have not used in testing. If you want, I can have them brought up for you to test. Sometimes, the way they die can be fun to watch." She turned to look at Brielle.

"Just offering, you know, one scratcher to another."

"No! It is wrong to kill our kind for…" He blurted out Pope Sophyra.

"Shut your mouth." Interrupted Phaedra.

"I make the decisions for this test!"

"Thank you, no. I have to leave now. Several of my guards will witness the burning." Said Brielle, looking from Phaedra to Sophyra and back again.

Sophyra looked disappointed at the announcement. But Phaedra's eyes narrowed. Her mouth opened as if she were going to say something, but she slowly closed it.

"How do we know you speak in the name of Lady Challis?"

"Challenge me, and you will find out."

"Very sure of yourself for someone so young," shot back Phaedra.

Abruptly, Brielle moved in Phaedra's direction, causing the latter to move back quickly, almost missing a step. The whites of Brielle's eyes flooded with blood, a sign she was ready to fight.

"Challenge me, and you will find out." She repeated.

Phaedra looked away but found herself looking at Sophyra. She hissed violently at her. She muscled Sophyra out of the way, and stormed towards the exit.

Canasta's small mouth made the sound of an outboard motor as she lay sleeping on the cushions at the end of the day bed. A full pale white moon hung low in the sky. Elect-Si stretched her legs from under her robe, being careful not to wake Canasta. Ounce comfortable she stretched out her hand for her glass containing a mixture of blood and brandy.

"Tell me again, I want to hear the details over and over." She said turning to Lady Challis.

Lady Challis inhaled the smell of her Scotch.

"Really, you sound as if you did when I told you a story when you were little. But oh well. If it will shut you up." Lady Challis bared her legs to allow the moonlight access to her thighs.

"Immediately after Brielle scratched me, I felt an intense tingling spreading through my entire body, but concentrating where my back and flying muscles were so tired and aching. It seemed to race down my arms and legs to my hands, fingers and toes. I could even feel my finger and toe nails. Which probably makes sense? I could see and hear more clearly." She paused to sip her drink.

"It even made the lips on my vagina tingle. I so wanted Burkhardt. I wanted him so bad!"

"I know, the entire palace must have heard you after you left to go to your room."

Lady Challis looked sideways at Elect-Si.

"Trust me, when you and Manuel are at it, we hear you."

"There was an incredible feeling of calmness in me, in my brain, in my heart. All my memories seemed to be sharpened and clearer." She paused.

"I have not told you this, but finally. Finally! Narmer's death and my departure from Egypt are clear now. I can look at our love and enjoy the times we had together rather than concentrating on his death and my leaving ... the aimless wandering that followed. The self-indulgent time I spent grieving is a brief moment at the end of the years of love and happiness we experienced." She looked up at the stars, as contemplating counting them.

"Those times are thankfully, closed." She opened the ice bucket on the floor and held up an ice cube. At the heart of the cube of frozen water, a small red ball of blood. She slipped the cube into her drink.

"The blood in that ice cube. That is all the blood I have wanted for days. That is another change I have seen in myself. Si, am I in danger of becoming a Vampire Goddess who does not drink, or even want to drink, blood?"

Elect-Si stared at Canasta; the outboard motor had stopped its rhythmic back ground sound. Now, her daughter was sleeping soundly. A deep sense of love for all she had brought into her life started to grow within her. Canasta could be annoying at times, actually, many times and her telepathic abilities continued to astound Elect-Si. The thoughts were fully formed and recently, they had become very deep in their probing for answers, the questions of which were often not communicated to Elect-Si. The back and forth with Canasta could be distracting and frustrating.

"I can hear what you are thinking mother!" With those words Canasta's eyes popped open and she rolled so that she was now facing Elect-Si.

"Annoying and frustrating. Is that what you think of my search for knowledge?"

"No! I didn't mean it that way?"

"Well, that is what I heard you think … better get off your ass, there are some people knocking at the gateway … they mean business."

Elect-Si froze, staring at her baby. But in the next moment she was rolling off the day bed and tightening the belt on her robe. She looked at Canasta who was vaguely pointing to her right.

Amun and Hades stood close to the wall, blinking at the brightness of the moon and looking around the world of the living.

As Amun stepped forward several Egyptian soldiers stepped forward behind him. Mean looking they carried Egyptian cycle shaped khopesh swords. Their muscular bodies were oiled so that any attempt to hold on to them, it would be very difficult.

As Hades stepped forward, he was followed by Persephone, the hand that had come close to Elect-Si's toli hung limply by her side. She was the first to see Elect-Si. She called out and pointed in Elect-Si's direction.

Amun turned, his soldiers lining up behind him.

"Gatekeeper!" He bellowed.

"We have come to force the gate. You must open it willingly to let the true masters of humanity come into the light."
Oddly, Hades raised his hand as if to stop Amun and the demands he was making.

"My beautiful wife, the Goddess Persephone has no use of her hand. Restore it!" He demanded in his rich baritone voice as he adjusted his toga.

Elect-Si reflected on how, in that moment, she realized she could understand each of the Gods, as they spoke in their ancient languages. She set the thought aside for later.

"If you leave now and return to where you came from, nothing will happen to you. If you do not, and I have to send you back, you will suffer for eternity."

Amun put his hands together as if in prayer. As he did so, the soldiers behind him rushed past him brandishing their cycle shaped swords above their heads, mouths open as if screaming blood-curdling battle cries. Except. No sound came out of their mouths. Their motion seemed uneven, there were noticeable limps in two of the soldiers, and one seemed to have problems with his sword arm as he was not able to raise it above his head as easily as his comrades.

Behind her, Elect-Si heard Amunet's voice.

"The soldiers fell in battle many millennia ago, broken shoulders, cleaved open in battle. Legs broken or cut off. The dead do not make sounds."

"Look out Mother," Elect-Si heard Canasta speak in her mind.

Elect-Si side stepped the first soldier's charge and swinging sword. As he struggled to stop his run she grasped his wrist tightly, oiled as the wrist was, Elect-Si found she had a perfect hold and twisted, shredding the forearm muscles from their attachment point at the elbow. Holding his wrist, she pulled it in front of him and towards the ground. The motion made him stumble. Elect-Si brought her elbow down hard on the back of the shoulder, breaking it and causing the soldier to drop his sword. She moved quickly to pick up the weapon and swing it at the back of his head, cutting it in two. The soldier seemed to shimmer in the moonlight and disappeared.

Out of the corner of her eye, Elect-Si saw her mother pick up Canasta and heard her call out for guards.

Elect-Si turned back to face the other soldiers who were seeing the first fall, had broken their charge and we were preparing to attack as a group. Instinctively, she raised her sword and parried a heavy blow coming to her from her right. Another single soldier had broken ranks with the others and was attacking separately. As he twisted away from her, to give him space and energy for a backhand slicing movement, Elect-Si punched hard at his exposed ribs and heard what she interpreted as the breaking of several bones. Then she brought her sword down on the back of his neck, decapitating him. The body and head shimmered and disappeared before they hit the ground.

Quickly, Elect-Si took the advantage moving rapidly towards the remaining soldiers. Behind her she heard her guards enter the verandah and the bark of an assault rifle. To her left one of the soldiers literally exploded like a fragile Christmas decoration dropped on a hard floor. Moving to the remaining two, she ducked as one swung his sword at her head. It passed over her but her sword separated his lower and upper leg. As she looked up at him start to fall in her direction, a spray of bullets ripped into his chest, he exploded into shards of what appeared to be glass and then everything disappeared.

Elect-Si stood up, there was one soldier left, the one that had not been able to raise his swords as high as the others. She moved to one side, causing him to move abruptly and into a better position for a burst of bullets that broke him into shards and disappear like the others.

Elect-Si moved sharply towards Amun. His face was a mixture of confusing expressions, one flashing on to it and the giving way to the next. Surprise, disappointment, and anger flashed across it. She stepped closer and he disappeared.

Elect-Si turned to Hades and Persephone.

"You, Hades, do you have anything to say?"

Making an effort to stand tall and fill out his chest, Hades's eyes narrowed.

"I am a god, you do not talk to me that way!"

"I am the gatekeeper; I will speak in any manner I chose. Do you have anything to say?" her words were met with silence. Hades's mouth opened and closed as if he wanted to say something but no words came out.

"No! Then get back to where you came from and take her with you."
Hades started to turn but met resistance from Persephone. He took hold of her arm and made her turn towards the wall and stepped into it and they were gone.

Elect-Si studied the sword. It felt solid, but it was made of iron. This was a New Kingdom weapon, before then it would have been made of bronze. It had an edge, but nothing like that of her katana. As she moved the sword in her hand, she guessed its weight to be between five and seven pounds.

Miray appeared. Elect-Si could see she must have been swimming or having a shower, her hair was wet and dripping, she was not wearing her trademark bandana, her uniform shirt and pants had water stains where she had put them on without towelling off first. She moved from guard to guard, setting up new stations and giving them new orders.

"We will talk in the morning," said Elect-Si.

As Miray left Elect-Si turned to look at her mother and Canasta.

"You kick ass mommy" were the simple words that came from her daughter. Lady Challis tried to hold Canasta closer and shield her but the baby pushed her hand away and twisted in her arms so that she could see and hear everything.

Lady Challis turned away from Elect-Si.

"Amunet, what was that? What happened?"

"The veil between the spirit world and the physical continues to grow thinner, more and more spirits are able to cross over, they grow more threatening."

"I agree!" It was the voice of Elect-Si's guide."

Lady Challis started to open her mouth to shout for the guards to come back as she heard and then saw him. But Amunet moved to stop her.

"It's alright, mother he is my guide. We have spoken about him many times." Said Elect-Si

"You can see me Lady Challis?"

He looked at Lady Challis and Canasta, then he reached down and tried to pick up a glass, it vibrated on the table top and then rocked back and forth as he tried several times.

"Your mother can see and hear me, but I cannot interact with physical things yet. Interesting."

"Who is that!" Exclaimed, Lady Challis.

"It is one of my spirit guides," she pointed at Amunet.

"Amunet is also a guide, to me, and to Canasta. Aren't you?"

Amunet looked from Elect-Si's guide to Canasta and back.

"Yes. I have that privilege." As she spoke, she moved to Elect-Si and placed her hand on Elect-Si's which held the curved blade. She moved her hand along the side of the blade.

"Iron. New Kingdom." She confirmed as she turned over to read the inscriptions on it.

"Cartouches from Thutmose III." She turned to Elect-Si's guide who was now standing next to her.

"It is not just the veil between the spirit and physical worlds that are thinning, it seems the different ages of existence mirrored in the spirit world are blending as well."

The guide looked at the blade pensively.

"Put it down on the table."

Elect-Si slowly walked over to the table and placed the blade on it. For a moment it lay there. Then shattered. The fragments disappearing like ice shards placed out in the sun.

" … and what about the bullets my guards fired?"

"While you are present, the guards can see them, and their bullets are effective. If you are not present, your guards will not see them, and not be able to shoot them."

"What the fuck is going on?" demanded Lady Challis in a loud voice.

"Careful," the word in Elect-Si's mind came from Canasta.

"Grandmother doesn't get it."

"Now that I have this Toli, this shield, I have the duty to be gatekeeper between the spirit world and the Now, this physical world." She paused.

"I understand that!" exclaimed Lady Challis annoyed at her inability to express herself.

"Well, some spirits, in this case, the Egyptian god Amun want to come through into the Now and enslave humanity again, to be worshiped and have temples built in their honour." Said elect-Si

"Amun and others like him will try and force the gateway that your daughter is guardian of." Added Elect-Si's guide as he turned to look at Lady Challis.

"Are we safe?" asked Lady Challis.

Elect-Si looked from Amunet to her guide and then met her mother's hard stare.

"Yes. We are safe."

Amunet looked at Elect-Si and then at Lady Challis.

"Si, is both the gate, and the gatekeeper. Things will happen around her when or if a spirit tries to come through into the Now."

"I will put Canasta in her crib, we need to talk." Said, Lady Challis.

"Don't you let her put me down?" shouted Canasta in Elect-Si's mind.

"If you do, I promise I will kick and scream all night," then the small eyes seemed to narrow.

"If you let her put me down, the next time you put your teat in my mouth I will bite and chew on it so hard that you will be sore for days,"

Elect-Si held out her arms.

"Give her to me, she will be quiet with me."

Canasta looked approvingly at Elect-Si and turned and put out a small part of her tongue at Lady Challis, who frowned in return. "Si, we should do something, they can't just come through from the spirit world like that. How about going to the spirit world and teaching them a lesson?"

Amunet inhaled sharply and turned to Elect-Si.

"You must not do that!" She exclaimed.

"The gateway is wherever you are, they cannot come through in another place, say the middle of Australia. If you go to the Underworld, you will take the gateway to them. That is what Amun wants. He is trying to antagonize you, to make you act rashly." She reached out and touched Elect-Si's arm.

"I know him."

"Yes. Amunet is right," joined in Elect-Si's guide.

Elect-Si looked from one to the other and started to relax. Out of the corner of her eye, she saw her mother walk over to the verandah wall.

"Mother?"

"Take it from a Mongol General. You fight when you want. You fight on the battle field of your choice. You fight on your terms." She paused and turned around to look at them.

"One of our most successful strategies was the feigned retreat. We started an attack, then we pretended to retreat, luring the enemy to follow us. At the right moment we turned around, and butchered them."

A grim smile crossed her lips. Her mind shimmered and she was on a battlefield. She looked down at her sword hand. The blood of her enemy run down the length of her arm and dripped from every finger like water. She dared not ease her grip on the handle, if she did, the red liquid would get between her hand and the sword, making it slippery and hard to grip. The sky was clear blue, bright and sunny, Tengri looked down on her, she knew he did.

Screams of dismemberment, death, and victory are surprisingly similar she realized as they pressed in on her senses. Why she thought of these memories she did not know. There had been so many battles this year. So many had died.

She looked down and tightened her grip on the sword handle anticipating resistance as she pushed the blade tip into the throat of a horse archer she had just unseated from his mount. He had been winded by the fall and lay on the ground far too long catching his breath. The tip met his spine and she leaned forward on the sword to crush those small neck bones. His mouth opened and he tried to scream but his throat was already cut, larynx crushed. Blood squirted from his mouth onto her chest and drenched her sword hand.

"Yes, we butchered them." She repeated quietly.

Elect-Si woke with a start. Canasta lay on her back on the bed between her and Manuel. She was bawling her lungs out. Her now not so small legs, feet, arms, and hands pounding on the bed.

Elect-Si was already sitting up, she looked over at a grunt from Manuel. Their eyes met, she shushed him back to sleep.

Instinctively, Elect-Si picked up her daughter. As soon as Canasta was in Elect-Si's arms, the crying stopped and her face looked up, she seemed pleased at the speed of Elect-Si's reaction.

"What is wrong baby?" she thought as she slipped out from under the covers and walked, half asleep to a large comfortable chair by the open verandah doors.

"I suggest you open your eyes and wake up. Walking half asleep, carrying your daughter, might make you bump into furniture."

As the thought ended, Elect-Si felt the violent assault of a coffee table. Her step faltered and she bit her lip to stop the cry of pain. But it fully opened her eyes and she saw the layout of the room clearly now. When she reached the chair, she sank into it, both holding on to Canasta and rubbing her leg at the same time.

"See! That will leave a nasty bruise. Serves you right! And you could have dropped me."

"What is the crying about?"
"Things are happening, changing. I need you to tell me what is happening to me."

"OK. What is changing?"

"My mouth, the top of my mouth itches, and feels as if it is on fire. It started tonight."

Elect-Si wiggled her little finger in front of Canasta.

"I have to put this in your mouth, I have to check something."

Canasta pouted at her.

"Have you washed it?"

Elect-Si frowned.

"Will this do?" she put her finger in her mouth and licked the finger.

"I guess it will have to do." The sigh, although in her mind, conveyed to Elect-Si a mixture of disappointment, and resignation to what was happening.

Elect-Si ran the tip of her finger along Canasta's lips and the baby opened them, letting her finger in. Yes, thought Elect-Si, poor Canasta's little mouth was on fire, but in a good way.

"Baby! Your fangs are growing. Soon they will fill those small channels in the roof of your mouth. After that, as you grow, everything will grow in step. This is just heat from them growing so quickly now."

Elect-Si took her finger from Canasta's mouth and pulled her closer to her as she lay back into the cushions. She could feel sleep start to slip through her mind.

"And!" Exclaimed Canasta.

"And what?" thought Elect-Si sleepily.

"My fingers. The ends are on fire."

Elect-Si lazily processed the thought and then sat upright quickly. She held the tips of her baby's pudgy fingers against her cheek. They were as ragingly hot just the same as the roof of her small mouth. She held the hand into the clear white light of the full moon coming on through the doors.

"No way! I must check with Brielle, I know you have fangs, but I think you also have finger nails like Brielle!"

A satisfying gurgling sound ripped through Elect-Si's mind.

"Knew it! I can bite and scratch!"

Lady Challis looked through the swirling smoke from her cigar. In her right hand a crystal glass of dark rum. Somehow, without any blood mixed in, it looked richer and darker. Gently she clinked the ice cubes against the sides.

"We never feigned retreat without first scouting and planning where we would turn around, and attack them. Si, if you are going to use the strategy, you, we, need to pick the killing ground." Her eyes narrowed in the direction of her daughter.

"What you are, and what you are planning is a bit out of my league. I only ever used this strategy against humans…. And a few vampires during the insurrection wars."

"Don't worry," said a voice from behind Lady Challis.

"It will work out." Amunet moved past clinking her glass of water with Lady Challis's glass. She walked sensually in long loose white Egyptian cotton pants held at the waist by a gold link belt. A tailored white jacket with a single button closing it. Her feet were bare. The fire dragon stood on her shoulder giving her the appearance of being very tall. She sat down opposite Elect-Si but looked at Brielle and Canasta.

Elect-Si only looked sideways at her mother. The words seemed not have made any impression, her eyes were on Canasta and Brielle. Canasta was growing rapidly, getting big and strong for her age. Soon, her daughter would be compared to children much older. Brielle was carefully and casually inspecting Canasta's small finger nails as she played with her younger sister. The entire tip of the baby's fingers was burning hot as if an infection were present.

Elect-Si put down Brielle's tablet. Her daughter had prepared a summary of Nazi research into fangs and enzymes forced from the young boy they had captured, mutilated, and was now dead. The research combined with the final pages from a letter the old man had left Lady Challis highlighted the futility of the research, the torture and mutilation he had been subjected to.

Vampire enzymes, whether injected in a bite, spat out, or delivered in a scratch could not be replicated for use as a weapon. At least as far as fanged vampires were concerned. Enamoured with the image of fanged vampires in Hollywood movies, the Nazi's had not looked for any other species.

Elect-Si was not surprised at the lack of attention paid to the possibility of other adaptations and variations of the vampire species. As powerful as her mother was, even Lady Challis was unaware of Sophyra, and Brielle's variants. Now, from her womb had come another. Or maybe Canasta was alone? Surely, in the all of history there must have been other crossings of vampire species. But how to identify them? What would they mean to the existing vampire species? Could there be a vampire out there that had all three ways of delivering enzymes?

"Si! I am talking to you!" Scolded Lady Challis.

Elect-Si's head moved slowly to face her mother.

"Sorry! I was thinking." She turned back to look at Brielle and Canasta.

"Canasta is very special; it is not the telepathy or that she was born aware. Canasta has both fangs and nails."

Hearing her name, Brielle looked up at Elect-Si and then Lady Challis.

"Yes, that is true. The raging heat in her fingers, it is normal for a baby with our kind of nails."

Lady Challis sipped at her drink as she looked over at Brielle and Canasta. She held up her drink and indicated to a servant that she needed a few drops of blood to be added. Slowly, she put her cigar into the ashtray and then rubbed her forehead.

"I really, really, never saw this coming."

Amunet turned back to look at Lady Challis.

"It will work out. Trust me."

"Why are you so sure?" Challenged Lady Challis.

Amunet stared at Lady Challis for several moments before replying.

"There is a small piece of your heart, your love that still belongs to those who are no longer with us…"

Lady Challis stared back and let the words enveloped her. She picked up her cigar and puffed it back into life. She looked at the now ragingly hot tip. As she exhaled, a word came with the smoke.

"Narmer…."

"You know what it is like to be treated as a goddess, sitting at the right hand of a man, a human who is worshiped as a god. So was the Great Khan and yet you loved him like a father. You saw him as a god striding across the Mongol Plain and you did all you could to please him without fucking him." She paused and sipped from her water.

"Sun Tzu said, if you know the enemy and know yourself, you need not fear the result of a hundred battles. Elect-Si, you know yourself, and you know me. We all know what Amun, and Hades want." She paused.

"There will be others wanting … pressing … to come through if we do not act…"

Brielle turned around from the veranda railing.

"You want him dead; you want Amun dead. As dead as anyone can be. He usurped you by claiming to be the masculine to your feminine. He claimed to complete your role in the universe. But you have, and always will be complete. You do not need a masculine entity to be all-embracing."

Amunet slowly raised her lips to her glass and sipped. The fire dragon stood upright and glared in Brielle's direction.

"Yes…" she said slowly. I want him dead for all the reasons you give. How?"

"In your waistband. You have a gold-handled dagger." Said Brielle as she stepped closer.

"It is the type used in your time for ritual execution. You would need such a blade to kill him. You are carrying it in case the gateway is forced open and he emerges. He must be killed in the physical world, in the here and now."

The fire dragon moved along the back of the chair to be closer to Brielle. Its eyes locked on hers. She moved another step towards Amunet. Slowly she reached out her hand in the direction of the fire dragon.

Elect-Si started to lean forward in her chair, her mouth opening to warn Brielle not to press the tolerance of the dragon, or, Amunet.

As she opened her mouth, the dragon moved its snout to Brielle's hand and nuzzled against it. Brielle, scratched the hard skin of the nose. It moved against her like a kitten against a human's hand. Abruptly it knocked her hand away. And moved backwards long the chair back to be with Amunet.

"You knew, didn't you?" Said Brielle to Amunet who was nuzzling the dragon's snout against her neck.

"Yes. Your pheromones. I was not familiar with the dragon in them but the message was clear."

"What!" Exclaimed Elect-Si.

"Your daughter was bitten by a Komodo Dragon. Obviously, she survived but its venom is still in her. Elect-Si, your daughter is not just a vampire who kills by scratching, she also has the ability to poison and kill like the dragon that bit her."

"Brielle" is this true?" Asked Elect-Si.

Brielle looked at her mother and shrugged.

"Yes." She paused and then slowly pulled up the sleeve of her shirt.

"We were visiting the zoo and shown a baby Komodo Dragon. I reached out to pet it for some reason. At that moment a boy pulled its tail and it reared up and bit me as if we're the one pulling its tail." As the sleeve moved up the teeth marks of a vicious bite were revealed.

"In the ancient past, before humans, those dragons flew and were brilliant, venomous, predators. They gave up flight when the dinosaurs that preyed on them died out." Said Amunet as she looked up at Brielle and then across at Elect-Si.

"Brielle is a most elegant predator."

"That is what I meant when I said Brielle is protected by something different but equally powerful." It was the voice of Elect-Si's guide from behind Lady Challis.

He walked past, stopping to smell the flowers and stand in the warm sunlight for a long moment.

"We are plotting." Said Elect-Si suddenly, the words seemed unexpected and her mouth confused by their appearance.

"I know. I also know Amunet has thought it all through, she knows what has to be done." He faded away as abruptly as he had appeared.

Elect-Si stared out from the high ground she stood on. The gateway between the world she was looking at and the physical world of her mother, Brielle, Canasta and Manuel was shimmering next to her. She ran her fingers along the glistening edge, it seemed too thin to be the difference between this world and her world, like a pane of glass. Nothing more. On one side was a world she wanted to preserve. She would fight to preserve. On this side a world that surprised her. Peaceful and quiet, many souls moved around it without fear or worry. This was not the fires of hell portrayed by Abrahamic religions. There was a wealth of knowledge and strength to be tapped into.

She could walk this world without fear, protected by her Toli, and all the power it brought her. As she thought of her heritage, her shamanic heritage, tingles ran up and down her body in waves. She was a white Shaman, but like the Ying and Yang, there was a black dot in the whitest of white halves, and a white dot in the blackest half. The blackness, she saw clearly now as the vampire in her and yet it was comfortable and at peace wherever it appeared in the symbol.

She rang her tongue over her fangs in the roof of her mouth, the comfort of the blackness amongst the whiteness gave her a unique ability, something no other white shaman had. She could use the blackness to fight, and kill.

To her right a mighty river started to ripple and the water lap more vigorously on the banks that contained it. In the far distance, to the east, the sun had just risen and shone down on the amazing wonders of man.

The pyramids of Egypt still stood as they had when they were built. Clad in white stone they glistened in a way the robbed out, decaying remnants in the Giza plateau could not. So, the river to her right, that was The Nile!

On a rocky outcrop on the far side of the river, the equally unmistakable silhouette of the Parthenon. Still strong and white and complete. Her sharp vampire eyes detected no erosion, no stains of mankind's pollution.

The sun grew higher in the sky, and now she could see the rivulets of water distributing the life-giving substance to the irrigation channels that fed the green crops.

Her guide had tried to tell her how she would be able to see the Underworld in both Egyptian and Greek at the same time. Like polarizing lenses on sunglasses, the glare of expectation would be shaded away and she would be able to see clearly. She would see that both existed at the same time but shaped by those who ruled it, Amun and Hades.

Where was her guide?

Storm clouds were gathering over the pyramids and Parthenon, huge dark clouds, lightening flashed down to the earth. Water in the river to Elect-Si's right was starting to foam as it was twisted one way and then another by strange spirals of wind.

Small Egyptian feluccas rocked on the surface and some had started heading to the river banks, their captains worried about the impending storm.

Out on the dusty roads between the fields she could see a dust storm rising from Hades in his chariot. He was viciously whipping the horses pulling it as he leaned forward, his eyes flaring and his mouth dripping saliva on their hind quarters. Persephone clung to the hand rail with her blackened hand. The skin tight over a now boney appendage. It looked like the claw of a vulture.

Persephone looked up the hill to where Elect-Si stood. Her eyes appeared as slits of hate and hunger for vengeance. Her lips curled in disgust as she urged Hades to even more urgent brutality of the poor animals, their hind quarters already starting to bleed from the whipping they were receiving.

A figure started up the hill without pausing for rest. Eyes focused on Elect-Si and the portal to the physical world.

Amunet's stomach pumped vigorously from running as she focused on the path up the outcrop. Behind her, Amun stopped and yelled curses at her, he stood with his arms outstretched, a Khopesh in his sword hand waving in the air. Locking eyes on Amunet, he brought the sword down in a mighty arc showing how he would behead her when he caught her.

Above him, Amunet's fire dragon fluttered angrily at the movement and breathed fire down on the ground just behind him to urge him to start moving again and to start climbing the outcrop.

He started to scramble, then stumble up the hill, taking hold of rocks and small bushes to help him. The sword was now a hindrance as it deprived him of a hand that could help him up the slope.

Suddenly, Elect-Si was aware of Hades arriving at the foot of the hill. The storm clouds arrived with him. A strong wind started to blow, the river was now angrily bursting its banks and spilling on to the grasslands on either side. Boats that had not docked at the river bank were in trouble, at least two she could see had started to sink. The men on board splashing helplessly in the water.

Lightning flashed again and Elect-Si could feel rain hit her face, a loud clap of thunder made her jump.

All around, Elect-Si was aware the temperature was dropping sharply. It was getting cold; skies were becoming dark; soon they would become black.

Elect-Si moved back to stand close to the gateway and hold on to its edge. She reached out and grasped Amunet's hand as she came over the last large boulder. She pulled her friend and guide towards her. Amunet was too winded to speak. Half bent over, gasping for air, Elect-Si pushed her towards the threshold of the gateway and turned her around so that she could face Amun as he struggled to cover the boulders Amunet had just crossed.

Amunet met the stare of her pursuer and straightened up, stepping into her regal self. She stepped back and placed her heel against the gateway. As she did, she looked up to her fire dragon and waved it to come to her.

It breathed one last ball of flame behind Amun to spur him on and then flew to her shoulder.

Elect-Si looked down the slope of the hill and saw Hades powering up the slope on his powerful legs. Behind him in his chariot, Persephone waved and shouted encouragement to him and vitriolic curses at Elect-Si.

Amunet stepped backwards through the gateway. As she did, she cursed Amun viciously. From the other side of the translucent gateway. She waved at him and made obscene gestures. Amun who was now just a few feet away, spittle from his mouth covered his cheeks and his chin. He grunted like some raw animal as he drove himself to spring through the last few feet. His eyes burned with anger and rage so deeply they seemed to bleed. On the slope and running towards her Hades had made up a lot of his lost ground, he was now getting so close. So close. So Close. This was perfectly thought Elect-Si.

From the corner of her eye, she saw Amun heal just feet from the threshold of the gateway. He lunged for the opening as Elect-Si turned through the gateway and closed it.

Above her Elect-Si could feel the air moving from the wings of Amunet's fire dragon.

The sunbed and chairs of the palatial patio where they lounged in the sun, planning this were smashed and broken. Guards were rushing to take up position, but under strict instruction not to engage with Amun.

A burst of flame erupted over his head as the Fire Dragon goaded Amun to get closer to Amunet. Amunet's sacred gold headdress glittered brightly in the sun. The gold belt around her waist shone like a ribbon of sunlight caught and made into something ethereal yet powerful. Elect-Si watched as Amunet pulled the ceremonial gold handled blade for executions from the sheath on her belt.

Elect-Si reached for her cane. It flew across the patio, crossing Amun's vision, distracting him.

Amunet disappeared from sight and reappeared a fraction of a second later in front of Amun, too close for him to use his Khopesh. His head and eyes had just turned back to her after following the cane. His sword hand seemed confused and surprisingly, he started to lower the blade as the surprise confused him.

Amunet drove the blade up from under the chin into the brain. Amun's body shook violently, he dropped his sword which rattled on the marble floor. His sword hand reached up for her hand and the handle of the dagger. But it gyrated strangely in the air and grasped nothing.

Amunet stepped a little closer, her eyes angry with vengeance. She cursed Amun's eyes, she cursed his body, she cured his soul and she cursed his manhood. She promised him eternal imprisonment for usurping her.
His hand tried again to grasp at hers but failed to touch it.

Amunet pulled the blade from his throat and brain and stepped back. As she watched him fall to his knees, she spat on him and cursed him again, cursed his life, and cursed his soul again with greater anger.

He fell forward.

Amunet stepped aside to let the body fall face first on to the marble. She dropped to her knees on his sweat covered back and plunged the blade into the back of his neck and vigorously moved it from side to side to cut the spine. As she pulled the blade out, she looked at the crude and bloody hole in the back of his neck. She spat into it.

She seemed to be making a decision.

She let out a long sigh and then leaned forward and took hold of his hair pulling his head back, exposing his throat. She placed the blade against the skin and pulled up strongly. In that one motion, she decapitated Amun.

She rubbed the blade against his loin cloth to clean it and the slowly stood up, holding Amun's head by its hair.

On the marble, his body started to shimmer and writhe as if in some grotesque death throw. Then, suddenly it was gone, fading from the physical world.

Amunet turned and stared at Elect-Si, a proud smile on her face as she held up the head.

"We should send this back to the Underworld, to Hades. A token of what will happen if he comes through." As she spoke, Amunet walked towards Elect-Si, her fire dragon taking up its perch on her shoulder. She looked to the patio wall. Elect-Si's guide nodded approvingly.

"Now would be good," said Amunet looking into Elect-Si's eyes.

Elect-Si opened the gateway.

For a moment nothing happened. Then Hades's, strong muscular hands and arms came though as if from nowhere. The fingers grasped at the air-like tentacles. Amunet put the hair she held into one of the grasping hands and the fingers closed on it like a vice. She jumped backwards. The hand disappeared with the head into the Underworld. A few moments of silence passed that seemed like years, then a powerful angry voice cursed loudly as if from some invisible sound system.

Persephone's contorted feminine voice screamed in the background like some ethereal backing vocal to Hades deep baritone.

Elect-Si closed the gateway. She turned to Amunet and the two hugged for several minutes, happy and relieved in the success of their actions. As Elect-Si let go of Amunet, she saw that she had been silently crying and brushed tears from her cheeks.

"Let's go down to the lake and swim, wash away all that has happened."

"I would like that," said Amunet.

Such a perfect family gathering!

Elect-Si looked around and saw everyone who was near and dear to her. What she saw armed her heart. Here under the large umbrella, her mother Challis, husband Manuel, daughter Brielle, and her gorgeous baby, Canasta. Amunet her spiritual guide and confident. Amunet had finished breakfast and was sitting back watching Brielle help her younger sister stand, and balance on two legs.

Canasta held the single finger offered by Brielle on each hand. The baby was not so much a baby anymore. Hands, arms, legs, and feet were all now well-defined and looked strong. Now was the time to cross over from being a helpless baby that needed to be carried to one that could walk independently. It had been later than Elect-Si expected. Everyone around the table had contributed time and emotional energy in helping her baby learn to walk. Elect-Si gave a wry smile, Canasta would have long sexy legs, like hers, she would be quite the desirable woman, men would chase her, few would make out with her. But still she needed Brielle's fingers to balance.

Elect-Si's vision froze. A sudden coughing from beside her brought her upright, had she really seen that? Was it an illusion? No! they were there in the golden sunlight of their breakfast.

Wings!

Silvery and shaped like Brielle's, they were grey but streaked with blue, and gold. They flapped in midair to help Canasta steady herself.

Canasta let go of Brielle's steadying fingers and looked up, smiling at her. The small perfectly shaped wings fluttered to help her balance and then slowly, carefully Canasta started to walk backwards away from Brielle in steps that were increasingly confident.

Canasta stopped and turned to look up at Elect-Si. In her mind, Elect-Si heard Canasta speak.

"This is why I did not walk for so long. My wings were not ready."

Abruptly, Canasta turned around and walked over to Manuel, her wings fluttering to steady herself, her stride lengthening and feet placing themselves on the marble floor with increasing assurance.

She looked up at him, he started to reach for her, to pick her up as he loved to do. She backed away, she looked as if she were concentrating. Slowly, her mouth opened to form words.

"Daddy!' the word as clear and precise. It was languid, breathy, mature, and sensuous in a way a young child should not be aware of.

"Please help me on to the chair, I want to sit at the table like the rest of the adults."

Manuel extended his arms again.

"Of course baby."

With a flutter of wings, Canasta walked towards her father. As he picked her up, he hugged her.

"Your wings, your voice, they are just as I remember Ximena."

In a moment the wings disappeared as Canasta hugged her father.

"Yes, they are… It is me in this young body!"

Brielle brought her finger tips to her mouth. Her eyes wide with surprise and a little caution.

"Canasta, can you remember Ximena?"

Manuel sat Canasta on several cushions so that she could sit right up to the table and see everyone, and be seen.

"Yes." The same mature, breathy voice said firmly.

"Ximena scratched Daddy many times during their passionate love making." She turned to look at Elect-Si.

"When they were in their deepest passion, she would spread her wings over the two of them like a tent. Then they would fuck violently inside that feathery home." Canasta winked at Elect-Si.

"Try spreading your wings over the bed next time, and see what it brings out in Daddy."

Lady Challis chuckled.

"What else do you remember Canasta?"

Canasta turned to look at Brielle and then Amunet.

"I remember you flying over our community several times. The breezes and winds when you were around being so strong, so very unusual." She paused and pulled a paper napkin towards her. Slowly, carefully she flipped it over so that it stood up like a pyramid.

"It was the time you left Egypt." She paused and pushed the upturned napkin around on her plate.

"Narmer…" she let the name roll of her tongue and slowly fade away.

Lady Challis's expression became fixed like stone, her eyes watered slightly but tears did not form. She stared at Canasta. For a few moments no one said anything, the rising breezes of the early morning pulled and pushed playfully at the canopy over the breakfast table. The sound of the material was the only thing heard around the table.

"Brielle. Explain!" Asked Lady Challis.

Brielle leaned forward smiling, and speaking to Canasta.

"It is said that some very rare adepts of our species can pass memories down from life to life either through the mother or the father. They say the memories are complete, and that the new born has attributes of the parent who is passing on the memories."

"Ximena's wings were grey with gold streaks." Manuel looked at Elect-Si.

"I guess the blue is from you. And yes. She scratched me often when we were making love. I thought nothing of it except one time she scratched very deeply. She said she felt more bound to me than she had ever been and that she had passed on a great secret." Manuel sighed.

"She never told me what the secret was. I guess now we know."

Brielle turned to Elect-Si.

"This is so fascinating, the memories, she passed them on to Manuel but how did she know he would marry a vampire of a different species. He could have married a human and the memories would have been lost."
Canasta played with the plate in front of her.

"She knew Daddy would not marry a human. The scratches delivered a very special enzyme that only adepts have. They prevented him from becoming enamoured with a human but she didn't know about other species of vampire." She looked sideways at Elect-Si as she finished speaking.

"Are you still my baby?" Asked Elect-Si cautiously.

Canasta turned fully to look at Elect-Si, she was clearly excited.

"Of course, you are. I love you so much and so does Ximena and all the others who are alive in me." Canasta stared at Elect-Si as her mouth slowly opened, two small fangs dropped down from the roof of her mouth. Then they folded back up and she closed her mouth. She smiled and gurgled; she was very pleased with herself.

"I am one of you, and I am also one of us," she said turning to Brielle as she wriggled her fingers in the air.

Brielle who was resting her head on her hands, stared at Canasta in amazement.

"Si, I always knew you would have the most astounding babies, but never like this." Lady Challis stopped speaking as a servant handed a folded piece of paper on a silver platter. Lady Challis opened it and frowned.

"The Pope is waiting in the grand drawing room. She wants an audience." She frowned.

"Well, she can ask for an audience, whether she will get one is up to you."

The blank expression on Elect-Si's face surprised her mother.

"Pope… Pope Sophyra… Sophyra. You know, the one that spits." Said, Lady Challis.

Phaedra sat cross-legged in a large comfortable chair by the open window of her suite. The stars were bright and clear, a moonless night sky. She looked for and recognized some of her familiar constellations. As a young girl, she had learned them from a boy from the next farm.

He was human and she had not come to understand what it meant to be a vampire. They had lain under the night sky and talked about the stars, the constellations and the great thinkers of history who had studied the stars and the planets.

Soon, the stars were just small sparkling orbs of light in the red haze of her orgasm. After the first time, they made out under the stars, that became the only reason to go and play at astronomers.

Carefully, she took the towel wrapped around a bag of ice from her face. The burning from the blow from her father had started to subside. She knew there would be a bruise there tomorrow, even with the ice treatment. She refolded the towel and pressed it with the ice to her crotch. As the cooling tool touched her roughly treated lips, her mind exploded into memories of the past.

Her father had discovered what she and the boy were doing and laid a trap in the hedge where the boy crawled through from his farm.

As she prepared to go out to play astronomers, her father had come up behind her and seized her by her pony tail and yelled at her. He swore and cursed her. He yelled at her, telling her what he had seen her do with the boy next door. He cursed her again and they dragged her by her hair out into the pasture and through the gate into the next field where she played astronomer.

She screamed when she saw the boy. He was half through the hole in the hedge that marked the boundary between his parent's farm and hers. Around his neck was a wire snare, it looked tight but the boy was still able to speak. He begged her father to let him go, that he did not mean anything by what they were doing.

It was natural for a boy and a pretty girl to make out. But her father said nothing.

Then the boy moved and as he did so, he screamed and tears ran down his face. That was when she saw one of his arms was caught in a metal trap. The type that springs closed when pressure is put on the release. Her father used traps designed to break a leg of a trapped animal and hold it fast in agony until he collected and killed the poor creature. He said the jaws that cut through the skin let the blood drain out. He liked to drink the blood of any animal he trapped in this way.

Above the boy a large wooden post rested against the hedge. Her father showed her how the wire snare was attached to the post. Tip the post over he had said and the snare would tighten and cut through the boy's neck. He would bleed to death in front of her. Perhaps, said her father, the boy would be decapitated.

She promised, the boy promised they would stay away from each other. They promised pitifully, they begged in tears, they begged and promised, they vowed, they gave oaths.

Finally, her father had cut the snare and opened the trap. The boy scurried back through the hedge to his home cradling his broken arm.

On the way home, in the field where she and the boy had played at astronomers, her father threw her to the ground, and used her. He was brutal, violent and unforgiving, unloving, uncaring in his movements. As he stood up, his shape over her was just a black mass, blocking out the stars.

As he did up his pants, he told her the way he had just used her was the way real men use women. He reached down and put his hands around her throat and for a moment she believed he wanted to strangle her.

Instead, he lifted her off the ground by her neck so that they faced each other. Her feet dangled in midair, making small circles as they desperately tried to touch the ground.

He told her to be ready for him, whenever he wanted her.

There would be no more boys coming to visit her, none to make out with, no young men would come to visit her. Only him.

He told her, when the time was right, she would have his children.

Then he simply let go of her neck and she had fallen to the ground and lay sprawled in a heap watching him walk back to their home.

Suddenly, she felt a cool breeze across her nipples. The surprise coolness closed the memories the way sunlight closes a night of stargazing.

She looked at the clock. She would not be leading dawn services with a bruise on her face, she needed rest and sleep. But the bed was not somewhere she could rest. It had become a dark space, inhabited by the spirit of her father.

She walked over to the bedding closet and pulled a comforter from it. She dragged it over to the chair she had been sitting in and threw it across it. She walked to the refrigerator and took out a carafe of blood and poured half a glass. She opened the cutlery drawer and lifted the tray of knives and took a small plastic bag from underneath and poured its contents into the blood. The powder lay clumped on the top for a moment and then sank beneath the surface.

Picking up a small spoon, she walked to the chair and wrapped the comforter around her and curled up on the chair to drink her magic cocktail. There would be no babies this month.

Slowly, as she lay wrapped in the warm lightness of the comforter, she sat back and fell asleep.

There had been a time when she saw the value and the opportunity of having one of the two Popes under her control. Lady Challis had never ascended to the papal throne and perhaps it was good that she had not. The irrational behaviour of Sophyra, Phaedra, and Dorion was past, almost forgotten. She and her husband had worked hard to end the supply of human bodies, the processing facilities that went with them, and the marketing of human meat.

On the other hand, their supply chain was still flowing its river of gold, diamonds, and very valuable rare earth metals. It hummed like a fine-tuned machine. The wealth of their species was now at staggering levels and Brielle's species benefited from the family connection.

In her mind, Elect-Si sighed. When Lady Challis had descried the plan for a female, vampire, Pope, the plan, the scheme of centuries had been a beautiful shiny bauble. Elect-Si had enthusiastically joined and participated in the plan. Now, with Sophyra as Pope, it was tiresome and boring. Discovering other species of vampire had been rewarding, and surprising.

"But you enjoyed sleeping with Sophyra…" mused Canasta.

As a guard opened the door to the Grand Drawing room, she heard Canasta's thoughts.

"Be patient with her. Treat her like a child, as you did me."

Elect-Si and Brielle walked into the Grand Drawing room. Elect-Si's jaw was tight and showed the flexing of muscles underneath the skin. Her demeanour was sour. Her feelings towards Pope Sophyra had grown cold. Very cold. Deathly, cold.

The opening of the Drawing-room door had been a revelation to Elect-Si. It seemed to show her that marriage to Manuel, and her baby Canasta was a new path on which she is to walk. She no longer needed pleasures such as Sophyra. Her coldness to her had been replaced by a new desire, a desire and need to manipulate Sophyra for the advantage of her species.

"Pope Sophyra, so glad to see," said Elect-Si with a forced smile on her lips.

"Vicereine, it is good to see you at such short notice. I felt it could not wait until next month."

Elect-Si extended her hand to Brielle.

"Brielle is here as well." In her mind she heard Canasta's voice.

" … and me, me too. Mention me!" Elect-Si ignored the insistent voice.

Pope Sophyra's gaze moved to Brielle, there was a small movement in her lips, resignation perhaps, that she had to recognize Elect-Si's daughter. Slowly, she nodded in Brielle's direction.

"It is good to see you again Brielle."

Elect-Si listened; Brielle did not reply. Now, Elect-Si's eyes moved from the Pope standing stiffly in her crisp white papal attire to a heavy aluminum trunk resting on one of the palace's carts used for moving luggage and furniture. The trunk looked solid, sealed, and very locked.
Elect-Si gestured to the trunk.

Pope Sophyra looked at the trunk with an expression of surprise, as if she had not expected to find it there.

"Yes." She said somewhat uncertainly.

Silence suddenly barged into the room and only the sounds of the birds outside now filed the cavernous space.

"Yes… Yes, it is," stammered Pope Sophyra. But she did not more or say anything else.

"Perhaps we should open it," suggested Brielle.

Elect-Si sensed something smelled. She stopped walking and focused her mind.

"You know that smell, so do I?" mused Canasta.

"Death"

Elect-Si looked around the room, then at Brielle, who was also starting to sense why they were there.

"Perhaps you should unlock it. I assume it is locked? Asked, Brielle.

Pope Sophyra seemed to snap out the reverie. She stood up straighter, her face became more relaxed and her shoulders seemed to ease from their stiffness. She now focused on Brielle. As she did her hand moved to her cleavage and two fingers disappeared between her breasts and emerged a few seconds later with a digital key.

She held it up as she might hold a goblet of blood during the sacraments and the dropped it on a nearby table. Then she feigned a small bow and moved close to the open doors and the verandah beyond.

In a moment, Elect-Si felt anger boil up inside of her.

"Ah… No! Be gentle, calm down!" It was Canasta's voice.

Elect-Si momentarily felt a spike of anger, this time not towards Pope Sophyra but towards Canasta for being so right in her assessment of how things should proceed.

Brielle picked up the key and studied it. She looked at the trunk. She breathed in and looked towards Elect-Si. They would never find out what was in the trunk if she did not open it, but could this be a bomb? The key could be the trigger. She looked over her shoulder at the back of Pope Sophyra who seemed relaxed and simply waiting. If it were a bomb, how would it look? The Pope of the Eastern Church dead, murdered in a palace along with any number of vampires. But then she remembered that vampires are a Hollywood fabrication. She straightened the key and pressed it down onto the digital lock on the top of the trunk.

A simple click followed by some sounds of mechanisms inside disengaging.

Elect-Si moved forward and rested her hand on the back of Brielle's arm and nodded that she knew what had passed through her daughter's mind. She bent down to open the lid.

Inside, thick insulation held a cloud of dry ice in place which now swirled as the warm air from outside stirred it up.

Then, in a moment, it was gone.

The frozen face of an old man, a gardener, fine grains of sand and pollen nestled in the deep, old creases of his face. The skin was sun died and leathery, deeply tanned from being outside for long hours in all weathers. Slightly sunken, half-closed eyes looked up at her.

Neatly arranged around the head, greasy salt and pepper hair, and a few trinkets. Where the larynx should be, a crudely cut neck, a butcher's knife, the blade and handle were old and heavily worn from misuse in the garden, not the kitchen. The blade and handle were encrusted with congealed blood. Just below the crinkly skin of the neck, a pair of strong hard-working hands used to deep levels of manual labour and effort. Hands, crudely severed from their body.

Brielle slowly nodded and closed the lid. She heard the locking mechanism reengage.

"Guard!" called out Elect-Si. Abruptly six or eight appeared, all with their weapons raised. Plastic face shields pulled down and their uniforms buttoned up fully. Plastic surgical gloves on their hands. Should Sophyra spit, it was very unlikely any of them would be caught by the venom. However, she was sure the Pope would be splatted over the floor by many, many rounds of precise gun fire.
She beckoned one of them over.

"Take this to Burkhardt, he will know what to do."

The guard nodded and took the key from Brielle, then wheeled the cart from the room.

"Such a shame…" said Brielle.

"Yes," said Pope Sophyra, slowly turning to face them.

"He was a pleasure to be around. He knew so much about everything that grows. I used to walk through the gardens with him to learn what was new, what plants had been in flower, which had fruit ready to pick and eat." She paused as if reflecting on the spirit that had been the man. She reached into a hidden pocket in her robes and pulled a gold cigarette case and opened it. She seemed confused at the selection of cigarettes, but eventually chose one. As the cigarette case disappeared back into her robes. A gold lighter appeared, and she lit the cigarette.

Elect-Si silently sniffed the air, Gauloises. The rich smell of the French cigarette focused her mind on what they did not know about the Pope. Until this moment, the Pope had always smoked cigars in her presence. They must do better at understanding her habits, and the possible weaknesses they could exploit.

"After Cassius, the turnover of priests in Phaedra's bed was prodigious. I could not keep up."

"You mean your spies could not keep up?" Challenged Elect-Si.

The Pope glared back, but finally nodded.

"Then she started having him. He was both the gardener at the seminary, and her father. Before becoming the gardener, he had a small farm. With no sons she had to learn how to emasculate the male animals, and other chores such as which animal to kill for meat and to sell in the local market. That is where those skills come from." Pope Sophyra pulled deeply on her cigarette making the end burn bright red.

"I think … no. I know he was trying to breed with her."

"What are you really here for?" asked Canasta in Elect-Si's mind. Elect-Si considered the words for a moment. A valid question, but the tone of asking had to be pitched correctly so it was not confrontational.

"What are you really here for?" The words came out, Elect-Si hoped they were pitched correctly. But, almost immediately she doubted whether they were. Yet the words were out, the tone, well it was what it was. Neither could be changed.

Pope Sophyra picked up an ash tray and rolled the end of the cigarette in it to shed the ash that had built up. She opened her mouth slightly, as if to start speaking and then closed it. Instead, she inhaled from her cigarette as she looked at Elect-Si.

"There is a new army … growing within the church. It started between Phaedra's legs." She let the words hang in the air.

Elect-Si quietened her sense of frustration.
"She was having them for pleasure and to scratch them and turn them into her species of vampire!" He blurted out Canasta in Elect-Si's mind. The words were followed by whoops of laughter and raucous glee. Elect-Si found it hard to contain herself. Canasta's voice in her head would soon enough be the

voice of her daughter when she was older. For now, the soft palate and small mouth could not manage all the words she wanted to say. Yet, in Elect-Si's mind, her voice was clear, bright and sunny, perhaps the mixture of several women from Canasta's past. Women who had known men and enjoyed doing so.

Elect-Si waited.

"Phaedra's kind out numbers us. They intend to take the Papacy. They intend to put Phaedra in my place."

Elect-Si pressed her lips together to stop from laughing. Canasta was quite carried away with what she had said and how right she had turned out to be.

"By us, I think you mean your species?" Asked Elect-Si.

"Yes! Yes, of course…" Pope Sophyra studied the last inch of her cigarette and adjusted her fingers so she could take one last pull on the Gauloises. As she put it to her lips, she looked over the cigarette at Elect-Si.

It was a stare Elect-Si knew meant there was more unsaid.

The tip of the cigarette glowed and as Pope Sophyra stubbed it out in the ashtray, she exhaled a large cloud of smoke.

"Has Phaedra asked you to renounce the papacy?"

"We have discussed separating the secular and spiritual roles of the position."

"… Let me guess, you both want the same thing, the secular power and wealth of the church. Neither of you care very much about the spiritual well-being of the humans you are supposed to serve." Said, Brielle.

Sophyra's head turned to look at Brielle, she seemed surprised that she was still present.

"Yes." Said Pope Sophyra slowly but with a hard edge in her voice.

"Killing Phaedra's father did not win you any points. I am sure she is oh so ready to kill you." Said Elect-Si. In her mind Canasta's voice was laughing hysterically.

Sometimes, Elect-Si reflected, as she looked at the floor, trying not to laugh with her daughter could be difficult!

Pope Sophyra scowled at Elect-Si and then at Brielle for good measure. Her eyes narrowed and for a moment she bared her teeth. Then, seemingly realizing what she was doing, she closed her moth and her facial expression relaxed.

"I did not kill him… None of my priests … killed him." Pope Sophyra reached into her pocket and pulled out the cigarette case again. She studied it as if she were going to have another cigarette but put it back unopened. She seemed unsure of what to say or do next.

She turned away and took a step towards the verandah, speaking over her shoulder she repeated.

"I did not kill him. But some of my kind did." She audibly inhaled before continuing.

"They sent the head to me … they sent a message that the rest of him had been eaten in some sort of ceremony to bring back eating of human flesh. There is what the humans call, a balance of terror within the church right now. Our two species are ready to go to war."

"And … the humans lose," said Elect-Si, changing her gaze to the far end of the Grand Drawing room. She was tired of looking at Sophyra, whether it was her face or her back, she was tired of this woman.

" … yet you slept with her." Mused Canasta in her mind.

"You need a conciliator," said Brielle.

Pope Sophyra whirled around. The speed and force made the long dress flare out; the side panels opened to reveal gold crucifixes from the waist to the hem. They glittered in the light.

"Why do you care so fucking much about humans? They are prey, they are food. Dorion was right they are like cattle. Do you remember that? It was not that long ago. We are the higher life form on this planet, all others are subject to us. To us!" Pope Sophyra's fingers flexed into fists.

"When we move out to the stars, we will be supreme there too." The words were powerful, energetic. A small dribble of spittle glistened as it left the pope's lips and ran towards her chin until it was scooped up and thrown away on to the floor by quick moving fingers.

"Do you know who killed him?" Asked Elect-Si as if the end of the huge open space would give her the answer.

Pope Sophyra slid the ash tray back on to the table rather awkwardly, ash and the cigarette butt spilled on to the table. She looked at it for a moment and then shrugged, to her it was just another thing that was not working out as she expected.

"There is a small group of my kind, I have no control over them. They are known to eat human flesh. They are responsible."

"They must have influence at higher levels in your Papacy to know of his connection to Phaedra?" Asked, Brielle.

Elect-Si turned back to face Pope Sophyra.

"Perhaps they did not know he was Phaedra's father. They just killed him because he seemed to be Phaedra's favourite. Why bring the head here?"

Pope Sophyra's eyes narrowed and again she bared her teeth. Elect-Si heard a whisper from Canasta.

"Her primal nature is so close to the surface. Good. We can use that to our advantage."

Pope Sophyra stood more upright, in doing so she projected a degree of authority, she seemed to be ready to speak but it was Brielle who interrupted.

"No one believes you! No one believes you had anything to do with it." Exclaimed, Brielle.

Pope Sophyra's shoulders visibly tensed, at her sides her hands again became fists. Tight balls of knuckles, sinew, and bone.

"No! They do not." Hissed Pope Sophyra.

"But you wish you had … killed him." Said Elect-Si slowly, carefully, as her mind worked through the possibilities.

"Had I known he was her father I would have imprisoned him; I would have used him to bend Phaedra to my goals. " Said Pope Sophyra with a cruel emphasis on her words.

"But this group forced your hand and now you two species are ready to go to war. All this with your own disunited and disaffected." Summed up, Brielle.

"We need a conciliator. We need you… You must fill that role." Breathed Pope Sophyra looking at Elect-Si.

"That is not why you are here; you are not convinced your species can win. You do not know how to fight a war with another species and keep humans from discovering what you are." Said Elect-Si.

"She wants sanctuary!" exclaimed Canasta.

"Only Sophyra and Phaedra know of a third species of vampire, and none of them know about me. I have fangs and finger nails."

Suddenly, Elect-Si felt like having a brandy and a good cigar to think this over. The taste was just palatable in her mouth.

"One night. You can stay for one night. There will be no communication from here. You cannot run the Papacy from here." Pope Sophyra's mouth opened and closed but no words came out. Her lips drew a hard straight line, but her fists unclenched and Elect-Si detected a lowering of her heart rate.

"Then you will evict me?"

"Yes."

Amunet glided into the dining room of Elect-Si and Manuel's suite. Barefooted, the elegant grey flannel pants floated just above the floor. A crisp white tailored jacket held closed with one button contrasted with the grey and her warm sunny tanned Egyptian skin colour.

As she arrived at the table, she slid the button open and the jacket opened up, it did not expose much of her cleavage but it did reveal a leather and gold belt with a beautiful scarab beetle clasp. She placed her iced water in the table and looked across at Elect-Si.

"Exactly how do you plan to evict the Pope?" she asked.

Elect-Si put the last part if her breakfast into her mouth and chewed as she studied the question. Slowly, gently, she put down her utensils and picked up her serviette to pat her lips free of crumbs, and other debris from her meal. She looked across at Manuel's empty seat and the remaining items of food on his plate. She reached across and picked up a piece of fruit and ate it.

"Do you have his soul?"

"Yes, of course, I have every soul of every being, human or animal that has died. They leave me when they reincarnate. Do you want to know what happened from his soul memories?" She paused for a moment, looking thoughtfully at the flowers on the verandah.

"He resists me. He is begging me not to sift through are memories. All he will give us is that he was garotted from behind while he was sitting smoking in one of his green houses."

"Phaedra likes to use garottes." Mused Elect-Si.

"It was someone who had a lot of strength, or, someone who really hated him. Emotion, powerful emotion, adds enormous energy to physical action. Love and hate are the two most potent in the physical realm. There was no hesitation, the garotte severed the head in one motion." Amunet fell silent. Her eyes closed in deep concentration.

"Another soul crossed over a few days after the gardener's death. Very troubled, in terrible pain. The pain was deeper than I have seen for a long time. It was the soul of a vampire, a vampire that spits. He had been poisoned by another vampire, one that scratches." She fell silent again, her face took on the look of someone in very deep concentration.

"The two species were trapped in one physical body; they struggled for control of the flesh."

"Amunet looked up at Elect-Si to see what the reaction was, then sipped from her glass.

In his hand, he is holding a garotte, it has been placed there by what seems to be a child's hand. Amunet inhaled and rubbed her forehead.

"He is looking up at a crucifix, I think he is praying but no words are coming out, the poison in him is burning away his ability to speak."

"Could the child's hand be a woman's hand?" Asked Elect-Si.

" … perhaps…"

"Can you see if he killed the gardener?" Asked Elect-Si. "Hands are holding his hands. They guide him and give his hands purpose and direction. They do not give him strength, though. His hands grip the garotte like a vice. They pull so hard, so hard the head comes off at the first try."

Amunet opened her eyes.

"The murderer was one of the men Phaedra has been sleeping with. She scratched him not knowing he was one of Sophyra's species." They stared at each other for several moments.

"Or Sophyra sent the priest to Phaedra for her to manipulate and use." Mused Amunet.

"Or, it could have been coincidence, Phaedra simply exploited the situation."

Amunet put down her empty glass.

"A soul cannot hide anything from me, they cannot resist me, but some try. They are so ashamed at what they did in life that they fight to keep it a secret. I will have the truth from the gardener soon enough. I will sift through the priest's memories."

"What is the gardener's soul hiding? If you had to guess."

"A relationship. A sour, painful, relationship. Anger." Amunet looked past Elect-Si.

"Wouldn't you agree?"

Elect-Si swivelled in her chair to look at who Amunet was speaking to. It was her other guide.

"Yes … a relationship that lasted decades."

Elect-Si turned back to Amunet.

"How old is Phaedra?"

"I have no idea; birthdays are only of interest to me when a soul has passed over. They can be important as a way of measuring a soul's progress along their life path in the physical realm."

"I guess you bring an important message?" Asked Elect-Si.

Her guide did not respond, instead, he reached for and picked up Amunet's empty glass. He studied it and then flicked his finger against the glass to make it ring. He seemed totally absorbed by the glass and the sound he made with it. He flicked the glass again and moved the glass closer to his ear to listen to the sound.

"Amunet said I was ready. Ready to experience the physical world." He carefully replaced the glass on the table and bowed to Amunet.

"You were right, thank you."

He turned to Elect-Si.

"Since I crossed over, many, many millennia ago, I have never touched or been able to interact with physical things." He turned to Amunet.

"Amunet has been coaching, helping me. Now I can flick an empty lass and make it sing like a new spring bird. Thank you."

Amunet smiled, and nodded to him.

"That's nice … now, what is the message?" Asked Elect-Si.

Elect-Si pulled the silk cord of her robe tighter around her waist and knotted it. She walked slowly into the living room of her suite, a crystal glass of rum and blood in her hand, she sipped from it as she moved slowly.

Her focus was in the open doors to the verandah. To her left, the sounds of snoring. She raised her glass and sipped more deeply. Manuel lay on his back on the couch, one leg dangling off it into the floor, his head nestled in deep cushions. On his chest, Canasta, the rapidly growing child emitted a surprisingly deep grunting sound as she changed her position on her father.

Canasta was going through her second teething. The second teething was all about her fangs. They were growing stiffer and she now had control over whether they extended or remained folded in their grooves in the roof of her mouth. The stiffness was probably enough to puncture frail human skin, but not that of an animal with fur, like a goat, dog, or calf.

Elect-Si and Canasta had spent a lot of time recently with her mother, Lady Challis. Although Elect-Si was Challis's daughter, she had come to her mother as a mature human, a human bitten by another vampire. When she went through what Canasta was going through, she had been an adult and able to speak and learn and understand in a way that Canasta found challenging.

Brielle had been an amazing daughter. Elect-Si felt closer to her than she had ever thought possible. Brielle had spent days, weeks even with Canasta, helping her understand how to care for her finger nails. Even at such a young age, she was learning her responsibilities and her uniqueness. A vampire that delivers enzymes through scratching must have amazing nails! The nails must be shaped, filed, and examined regularly. Such a vampire cannot find themselves in a situation where they want to scratch only to find their nails are incapable of delivering their deadly liquid.

Elect-Si ran her tongue over her fangs. The thought of them and the liquid they injected had set in action a small, but steady flow of it into her mouth. The sugary liquid was a complex mix of enzymes and she could sense her body analyzing and breaking down each of the components.

This was an essential act for every vampire. It should be done regularly as life circumstances changed. Even the time of year could influence the enzyme mix along with diet, age, and, of course, the intention of vampire creating the cocktail as they bit into their prey.

It was the prey to die instantly, slowly, in agony or peacefully. Was the flesh to decay quickly after death, or slowly putrefy. A clear message to other vampires who might try hunt in the same area.

It was the prey to be a regular source of blood and nourishment and therefore locked to the vampire who bit them. If so, another vampire biting them would receive a painful, foul taste, and be warned off that prey.

Would the enzymes create a new vampire? A bite that changed the composition and life path of the one bitten was the most complex cocktail of all.

Perhaps there was one more complex enzyme blend. The one Challis had used to wipe away all traces of the vampire count who had first bitten her brooded Elect-Si.

There could be no laziness in understanding the chemical mix injected into prey. A vampire must test constantly what it was they were producing, and always match the mixture to intention.

As she stood there, the sugary taste evolved and changed. For a moment, it took on the taste of bitters, and then almonds. Each taste represented a balance of enzymes in its own right, breaking them down and remixing into a new cocktail with specific possibilities and use was so vital.

Then the taste changed back to a sugary sweetness but with a hint of berries, almonds, and still bitters. The perfect balance to give a human or animal, a quick death.

Motherhood had made many changes in her body, her enzymes, her venom as Gwendoline jokingly referred to it, was stunningly more potent now, and she could feel her fangs becoming harder, and sharper. Harder and sharper meant she could bite more deeply, with less effort, and inject more enzymes into the tissues beneath the skin rather than simply just under it.

Now when she wanted to extend them, they did so with the speed a lightning storm could not match.

Her Toli was different.

She had known and felt it envelope her heart. The core part of her being. But now it protected her completely in every way. It was at the tiniest … most minute level of existence. Scientists had long dealt with the subatomic particles that made up the atoms of all existence. She gently bit her lip. Science had been fascinating, she enjoyed the subject, she had spent hours drawing on scraps of paper, the protons, neutrons and electrons.

Science had taught her that these particles were "fundamental" and that they could not be broken down any further, how wrong science was. There were so many layers, so many levels below those particles. She had never guessed that someday she would be able to see them, even to spin an atom on its axis as she did now.

In all of them, everywhere she looked, her toli looked back at her.

Humans built huge machines to experiment on this unique and beautiful world. Why did they labour so hard when all they needed to do was ask her?

She could see … sense, and decompose every atom, every molecule passing into and out of her body in any form. Air was so rich and made up of so many different things, she could see and choose to allow some in, or, keep others out. Keep out the fragments of dirt suspended in the air but allow in the molecules of scent from the flowers so that she could revel in the beauty of their smell. She held a molecule of scent and luxuriated in every fractal of its odour.

In her stomach, she looked at the platelets of the blood she had just ingested. She flipped them over as a chef would flip over pancakes on a griddle so that she could see all aspects of them. Ah … one is slightly malformed. Gentle, she moulded and transmuted the platelet into one that was properly formed.

Her senses moved back to the air passing into and out body, she could audit the difference between what she breathed in and what she breathed out. But everywhere was her Toli, it protected everything, and it gave her powers she had never imagined.

It was in her very soul, her spirit. For the first time she could see her soul, her spirt as essential essence, she could walk up to it and look at them and they looked at her as two people might on the street who were familiar with each other, but had never seen the other before. She held out her hand and her soul mirrored her action. The finger tips were separate for a moment and then blended together. She held out her other hand and her spirit mirrored the action. Again, the finger tips were separate for a moment and then blended together.

She smiled, this was the best of all the changes, it meant so much. As an immortal being no other level of unity could be possible, she felt such peace from the union.

"Wonderful, isn't it?" said a pleasant girl's voice she was very, very familiar with. Emma.

The girl sat on the stone railing, nestled amongst the riots of flowers. Elect-Si stepped forward so they could hug and be close together.

"It is so good to see you!" whispered Elect-Si in Emma's ear.

"It is so good to see you too. You must come to the upper world, the tree with all the fruit is heavily laden, you would enjoy all the fruits it is bearing. I think it is doing everything just for you. Then, I will show you the village you can see from the tree."

"I would love that."

"Can you do something for me?

"Of course. What is it?"

"Your Shaman's staff, the cane as you call it. It needs a little energy."

"How do I do that?" Said Elect-Si as she took hold of the diamond handle.

"Hold it in the middle with one hand and place the tip against the palm of your other hand. Watch"

Elect-Si did as she was instructed. Slowly, in her hand a swirling maelstrom of purest, deepest black and brightest, whitest white started to form. As it grew in intensity, it swallowed the gold tip of her cane and spread up the shaft to the diamond handle. The diamond glowed for a moment and then started to radiate pure white and pure black light. Like a light house guiding and guarding sailors on the sea, the diamond appeared like a light house of purest darkness and whitest light.

"Wow!" exclaimed Emma.

"That is something extraordinary, I have never seen light that pure. I never thought to see the essence of light and darkness." Their eyes met.

"You really are from a time when nothing existed, not the universe, nothing. Only white and black light."

"That is my Toli. I did not exist then."

Emma frowned.

"I was with you when you looked past the subatomic layers of existence that humans talk about. I was with you when you looked at all the levels below what they are only barely grasping. I saw you touch and join with your soul, and your spirit, in a way no yogi, or spiritual human could contemplate."

Elect-Si looked at the cane, it had a spiritual presence in the physical word that had not been there before. There was a unique but familiar essence.

"Your Shaman's staff … cane as you call it. It is now as protected and powerful as you are. That is where I exist. That is where I will always be. We will always be together through time and existence. Look!" Emma reached out and threw her arms around Elect-Si's neck. Together they hugged.

"Look!" she repeated.

Elect-Si's vision changed. She was standing next to the tree with all the fruit. She reached and picked a pear and from the same branch she picked an orange. Emma knelt on the ground picking strawberries. In the distance, the roof tops of the village Emma had promised to show Elect-Si.

"Look down," breathed Emma as she handed Elect-Si some berries.

Elect-Si looked down and it seemed as if she were standing in midair, but she was not afraid. Beneath her the tree disappeared through the soil, its roots expanding outward in all directions. All of a sudden, she could make out the Lower World and then the Underworld.

"This, here, where we are, is the Upper World. Isn't it?" Asked Elect-Si as she ate.

"This tree, with all the amazing different fruits on the same branch. This is the Tree of Life. This is Ash Yggdrasil—The Norse World Tree." Elect-Si looked up the fruit-laden branches, so many different types of fruit all mixed together on the same branches.

"The Tree of Fertility," mused Elect-Si.

"It is all those things, and more. Perhaps you need to see it as The Tree of Knowledge." Said, Emma.

In a moment the fruit became tablets, their screens scrolling with information and knowledge. Scrolls of papyrus in all languages that have ever been written started to drop to the ground and unravel.

"This is my favourite." Said Emma stooping to pick up a scroll.

"Nordic runes. Read!" she said excitedly.

"I don't know runes…"

"Yes. You do… Read!"

Elect-Si took the scroll and looked at the strange writing and then it started to flow and became a Nordic Saga. It was complete with heroes and heroines, Viking long ships and voyages of discovery. Sea became land the Vikings had discovered… Amerika. She saw the powerful blonde-haired Norsemen and women shake hands with local Indian people and put away their battle axes and knives and sit down and eat together.

"I am keeping this scroll; I want to know how the saga ends.

"Said Elect-Si smiling at Emma.

"It is a good story, trust me. You will like it…"

A molecule of scent from the verandah flowers touched Elect-Si sense of smell and she was back on the verandah with Emma.

"Look." Said, Emma.

"What is this? Where are we?" Blurted out Elect-Si. The verandah had disappeared and she appeared to be standing with Emma and her cane looking out over a vast and never-ending plane that extended in every direction. Everything in front of her was dimly lit but clearly discernable.

"Look behind you," said Emma as she held Elect-Si's hand and turned her around.

Behind Elect-Si the vision was very different, it was like a vast tunnel disappearing into darkness. Elect-Si could see bright and colourful patches of paint … no, it could not be paint! It was on the walls and hung like strange islands in midair.

"Existence. That is what humans refer to as the past. It is what has gone and which they may be destined to repeat. They see it as linear … of course it is not linear. It is linear to them because of their limited ability to comprehend it. The bright colourful patches are beautiful things that happened in the past. The black patches, those are the bad things that happened. If you want, we can walk back through past existence?"

"No, not now," said Elect-Si turning back the other way.

"I am in my robe; I have nothing else on.

"She turned to look back where she had been looking first.

"Is that future existence?"

"Yes. It extends in every direction because there are unlimited possible outcomes from every action, thought, word, or deed in the NOW. The NOW extends in every direction because every moment in the NOW is a result of every moment in the past. Where we are standing is a moment in the NOW where you need to be." Emma waved her hand in the air as she drew close to Elect-Si, she held Elect-Si's hand and gently pulled at the fingers, then she stopped at the thumb and stroked it instead of pulling at it.

"Did you feel that?"

"Yes, of course."

"You are a White Shaman… You are The Gatekeeper. There has never been an immortal gatekeeper. There has never been a Shaman, one who understands the Great Spirit. No one is both pure whiteness and pure blackness. None as protected as you." Emma paused.

"When you
healed my arm, to do so in spite of the curses and threats by the black shaman who cut it off. The purity of your blackness is deeper than they can ever be and you do not know fear in its use." Emma squeezed Elect-Si's hand and smiled.

"The Gatekeeper is always in the NOW. You can move into the past, anywhere in the past, and you have some abilities in the future … not many. You cannot go into the future and change it." Emma pointed back to the tunnel of the past.

"Watch the birds flying, they are Geese. There are only a few that emerge from the past… See, how easily they fly through the NOW. Look how big the flock has become. They have prospered, they are breeding strongly. They are well fed; things are good for them."

They watched in rapt awe as the flock grew. They appeared to be flying over a mighty river. The flock grew again just before it moved over the boundary from the NOW into the future.

"What happened … the flock is smaller in the future." Said Elect-Si.

"A lot smaller."

"That river they are flying over, that is the Nile. When we saw them come out of the past, there were only a few. Mankind hunted them, they were food, their feathers were collected for pillows and cushions. Their eggs were taken to eat. As the population of man grew, more and more birds were killed. But then, man cultivated and raised crops and reared animals for meat, they hunted the Geese less, and less. The flock grew big." Emma stopped and looked up at Elect-Si. Their eyes met.

"In the future, there are fewer Geese, it could be disease, a new predator, pollution. Destruction of habitat. There are so many reasons."

"Is that why the future is all muted and shaded?"

"Yes. So that you cannot see the outcome of any action. To humans, what we see as muted and shaded, they see it as impenetrable blackness." She looked down at Elect-Si's feet.

"Step forward, just a small step. But step."

Elect-Si looked at his feet and shuffled forward a few inches. All around her things changed. Brightness appeared in one direction to her right and other places became lush and green with waving grass and grazing animals in a layer below, and to her left.

Behind Elect-Si, there was a sudden dark rumbling sound. Elect-Si seized her cane and whirled around. She brought her cane up as if to use it as a club. All that she heard and felt told her of a threat.

In the tunnel, the pounding hooves of horses rumbled and a chariot with Hades and Persephone emerged from the dimmest and darkest part.

"Tap your cane on the ground… Tap your cane on the ground… Tap your cane on the ground…" repeated Emma.

Elect-Si looked at her guide and lowered her hand and took hold of the handle and tapped the gold tip on the ground in front of her feet. The ground did not move or change but ripples of purest white and blackest black spread out like waves from a stone thrown into a lake. They spread under the horse's hooves, scaring them and making them rear up. The wheels of the chariot screeched to a halt, almost shedding the occupants on to the ground.

Hades waved his sword above his head and Persephone rained curses in Elect-Si direction. Her hand which had come close to Elect-Si's toli appeared grey and strong now rather than black, old, and withered.

"Hades, you cannot go any further," said Elect-Si.

"You are Gatekeeper between the physical and nonphysical worlds. You have no right to be here. No right to stand here in time. You have no right to stop us crossing into the future." He bellowed.

Elect-Si looked down at Emma and then at all around her.

"Yes, I am gatekeeper between the worlds. I am also gatekeeper of time, of existence. Where I stand is the NOW, it is that moment, that space between the past and the future of all possibilities that are yet to come."

Hades picked up his whip and tried to urge his horses forward but they resisted the brutal whipping. Persephone moved closer to him and held on to his arm and his belt. She pulled at his arm and Hades slowly put down his whip.

"I judge you. Neither of you can cross into the NOW. Neither of you can cross into the future. You must return to where you came from. Return to your time. To the past. Your time has ended; you cannot change that. I will not let you change that. Go back to it, and enjoy it. I bind you to adhere to its boundaries." Elect-Si paused and looked at the couple.

"I will know if you breach your allocated time. If you do, I will come and enforce my judgment."

Elect-Si, without realizing it, tapped the tip of her cane hard on to the ground. Shock waves, not ripples shot out from it. The waves of energy growing bigger and bigger as they moved backward through the NOW towards the chariot. Suddenly, the chariot, horses, and occupants were picked up and thrown back into the immense tunnel of the past. The chariot turned over and over like some strange toy accompanied by two children who had been playing with it.

"Are you OK?" Asked Emma leaning forward on the railing to look into Elect-Si's eyes.

"Yes. I think so. So much newness. So much to learn. Where do I get the words from?" Breathed Elect-Si.

Emma smiled.

"You get them from your heart. You were always destined to be the Gatekeeper you are fulfilling your life path purpose, your existence."

"To the end of time?"

"You will look back on the end of time and carry on … you have heard those words many times. It is true. Time means nothing to you, it never will." Emma paused.

"You are doing so well at all of this." Emma kissed Elect-Si.

"It is time for me to return to my place. So much of it will be new to me as well. No worries, we will visit often. Now you know what the tree is, you will be back."

Emma faded away from Elect-Si's vision. Instinctively, she reached out for her cane. It moved instantly to her hand. As her fingers wrapped around the diamond handle, she felt the comforting purr of Emma's spirit. The cane felt new, vibrant, dynamic … above all, it felt powerful. Enormously, powerful.

Elect-Si's hand drifted to her stomach, her womb. In the palm of her hand, she felt the electricity of a new baby growing in that warm basket of love. To have another child was not a conscious decision she and Manuel had simply not taken any precautions. Here it was.

As a vampire she had the ability to sense, and then change the sex of a child during the earliest stage of its forming. With Canasta, she had not tried, this one would be no different.

Elect-Si felt a draft as her robe was pushed open and then she felt Canasta's hands on her thighs. She backed away so that Canasta emerged from under her robe.

"Don't do that, it is rude!"

"Why, because you have nothing on?"

" … yes!"

"I got tired of sleeping on Daddy's chest. It is hard. I like sleeping on your chest, your breasts make great pillows."

Elect-Si pulled her rob tighter around herself and retightened the belt.

"They are not, pillows!"

"I know I sucked on them log enough, remember?"

"How is my sister?" Asked Canasta.

Elect-Si picked up the crystal glass as if she were going to refill it.

"I have not seen Brielle since yesterday, I have no idea how she is."

"No. Silly. The one in your belly!"

Elect-Si looked down at Canasta. How could she know of the pregnancy or the sex of the baby? She didn't even know.

Canasta giggled.

"I may be small I may be young, but you know … you know I have the memories of all who have been before me. I know what penises and vaginas are. I know what it is like to come!" Canasta paused and winked at Elect-Si.

"I can't wait for that…"

Canasta's face grew serious for a moment.

"I hear you and Daddy screwing … that is the right word…" Her small face cleared suddenly as she fell into deep thought. Then her face broke into a wide smile.

"No! Fucking! That is the word I am looking for. You two do it like animals, and, so often, so loudly." Her face changed again into one who appeared to be wise and knowing.

"I can smell your pheromones, that is what I was doing under your robe. The baby will be a girl." In a very mature gesture of stop! Canasta held up a hand.

"I know you can change the sex of the baby. Please don't."

"If that is what you want?"

"Please, don't mess with her. Let her come out all natural, as I did."

"Are you sure that is what you want?" Asked Elect-Si.

"That is what I want."

"OK, then I will not change the sex."

"For sure?"

"Yes, for sure."

"For double sure?"
"Yes, for double sure."

Elect-Si looked at the glass, she looked down at Canasta who seemed to have grown overnight.

"So, as you get older. Maybe now is the right age, you can try some blood. Do you want to try some?"

"Yes, Mommy. Please."

"OK. Let's get you some blood. Just a little of each blood group. You can find out which you like best." Elect-Si nodded in the direction of the door back into her suite.

"Come on…"

Lady Challis stood up from her chair suddenly. The straightening of her strong legs sent her chair spinning backward until the rear legs caught on something and it fell over with a loud crash.

In her throat the guttural rumble and piercing hiss of violently, angry, vampiric warning started to build as her lips parted.

Servants rushed to create a wall in front of her with their bodies.

Blue LED lights on every electrical outlet and light fixture started to silently flash an alert.

The heel of Elect-Si's hand caught Pope Sophyra's septum, that small, easily broken piece of cartilage in the nose that separates the nostrils. And broke it like a twig.

Pain and blood gushed from the Pope Sophyra nose, covering her nose and mouth, she screamed. A hand started to move up to her face to cover the bleeding, broken space as more blood gushed down, and into her open mouth.

Elect-Si's other hand came across in a true south paw's hook and smashed into the jaw, pushing it so far out of alignment with the face that it made the Pope look like a grotesque, weathered, gargoyle.

Brielle pirouetted on the ball of one foot. The other, leveraged by the uncoiling of her body, and the spinning of her weight in the opposite direction, slammed into the Pope's diaphragm.

Pope Sophyra crashed to the ground, gurgling blood, winded, and unconscious.

All along the great room, doors crashed open as scores of guards rushed in, weapons raised.

Silence.

Lady Challis slowly crouched down and smoothed the hair of the servant who had borne the brunt of Pope Sophyra's assault. His eyes moved frantically from side to side in their sockets as if he was desperately searching for something. His arms, legs and hands were rigid and contorted by muscles locked in their own painful, violent spasms. Blood started to run down his face from the corners of his eyes.

He started to convulse.

Lady Challis held tightly to him and started to open her mouth and extend her fangs. She wanted to give him relief, freedom from the pain that surged within his body.

Brielle knelt beside him, opposite Lady Challis. She pulled open the man's collar.

"This would be better." She slowly, deliberately, deeply, scratched the man's neck.

As if mesmerized by the action, Lady Challis stared at the scratch mark. It was reddening, the skin slightly red. It looked simply innocent. Her fangs retracted; her mouth closed. She looked from her granddaughter to the servant and back again.

"Thank you!"

Between them, the servant's convulsions slowed and then stopped and his limbs relaxed. He coughed. Slowly, his eyes stopped their spastic movements, and closed.

As Lady Challis stood up, she looked at Burkhardt who had just arrived. He stood in front of her breathless, deeply concerned. Miray stood behind him. Lady Challis pointed at the servant's limp body.

"Cremate him at midnight, with all rights. I will be there, she looked around at Brielle and Elect-Si.

"We all, will be there. Full rights for a valiant, courageous vampire warrior!" she turned to look at the unconscious Pope Sophyra.

"Take that to the hospital. Have the surgeon removes the glands in her neck that produce her venom." Lady Challis inhaled deeply, her stance and demeanour noticeably relaxing.

Miray started to move forward but a servant interrupted her.

"M'lady, I suggest we all move to another room so that this space may be purified according to the ritual."

Lady Challis smiled thinly, and nodded.

"Why did she do it?" Asked Elect-Si as she looked into the eyes of her Banjhakri. Brielle leaned forward from the rock she was perched on to hear the answer.

He stood there, shifting his weight from one foot to the other for several minutes as he contemplated the question. Slowly, he rubbed his stomach, finally picking a flee from the long fur and immediately putting it in his mouth to eat it.

"Provoke. She wanted to provoke you."

"Is that the answer?" mused Brielle.

"Is that all of it?" She asked.

The Banjhakri smiled at Brielle and then at Elect-Si.

"Your daughter is very intelligent. She asks good questions."

He plucked another flee from his fur, it met the same fate as the first.

"No!" His face spread with a smile.

"No. She was hoping you would kill her Elect-Si. She wants to die." He smiled and seemed pleased with his divination of the situation.

The Banjhakri eyes glittered brightly as they moved from Elect-Si to Brielle, and back.

"Who killed the one whose head I can see in a box?" He nodded vigorously.

"Who has made the Pope believe that her death is for the best?"

Brielle and Elect-Si looked at each other.

Suddenly, the Banjhakri became very animated. He waved his hands and moved around in a circle on his backward facing feet.

"Samurai… Samurai… Samurai," he repeated as he walked in a larger circle.

"What did they do when all seemed lost? I ask you both, what did they do?"

Brielle pulled her knees close to her face and rested her chin on her knees.

"They committed Hari Kari, suicide by disemboweling themselves."

"What? What? I cannot hear what you say. Do not mumble!" he exclaimed.

Brielle stretched her legs in front of her and looked directly at him.

"They committed Hari Kari, suicide." She said clearly.

The Banjhakri clapped his hands and smiled broadly.

"But … but … now, how different?"

"She wants to die but she does not have the strength to kill herself. She wants another species of vampire to kill her."

"One that is close to Lady Challis." Said Elect-Si.

"Yes… Yes … and…"

"War … war between species."

"No… NO!" He stood very still and flapped his hands in the air as if batting away mosquitoes.

"You think too much like humans, always going to war." He mimicked the blowing of a trump, and slashing with a sword.

Brielle smiled at the play acting.

"Cold war, war without blood spilled directly, spilled through proxies?"

The Banjhakri rubbed his eyes.

"The Head. It has a message, but you do not see it. Your eyes are closed and your mind sleeping." Finally, he sighed and looked again at Brielle and Elect-Si.

"Now, can I fuck one of you?"

Burkhardt looked down at the large, well-buttered slice of rye bread and started spreading slices of well-cooked crispy bacon across it until the butter was hidden. He turned his attention to the next piece of bread to be buttered and covered it with the golden richness. He flipped the slice over and aligned it with the one carrying the bacon and dropped it.

Then he pressed it down.

Then he cut the bacon sandwich into two manageable halves.

He brushed back a long strand of hair and stared for several minutes out at the rich scene he saw outside. Northern India, this palace was definitely catching and holding his attention.

He picked up one of the sandwiches and started to eat. The sandwich was deeply satisfying.

He heard Elect-Si put down her utensils and the gentle fall of her serviette on the table. The swift movement of a servant taking away her plate and leaving her with a large mug of steaming coffee. The coffee smelled so good.

He pushed the last bite of the first sandwich into his mouth. He brushed away the strand of hair again. He hated that strand but one of his wives insisted that it made him dashing and more lovable. He did not concur.

He looked across at Elect-Si, sitting in the chair at the head of the table. Her hands hanging loosely off the end of the arms. She looked relaxed, pregnant, but, relaxed. He watched as one hand drifted to her swollen belly, rubbing it, comforting the fetus inside.

"I had forgotten how beautify this view of the valley and the Himalayas are. You eat here every day?"

"Yes, mostly. You knew what you were doing … making me marry those two, being father to the children."

"Yes, I did. Didn't I." Elect-Si turned her attention to Burkhardt.

"The traditional option, you would not have liked, you may complain now, but the other you would have hated it."

Burkhardt pushed the end of the second sandwich into the remaining egg yolk on his plate and moped it up, then he bit down on the sandwich.

"Yes, I suppose I would have."

"The head."

"Yes. The head." Burkhardt took another bite, and chewed.

"I had it defleshed to the bone. He had fangs, he was one of us, a fanged vampire."

"Are you sure?"

"I had the fangs preserved and a small quantity of his enzymes left in them." He nodded to the tablet beside Elect-Si but she did not look at it.

"Anything in the enzymes of interest?"

Burkhardt pushed the last bite of his sandwich into his mouth and chewed. He sat back allowing a servant to clear his breakfast things and put down a mug of hot steaming Turkish coffee. He cradled the cup as he finished eating and swallowed.

"Spill it, tell me what you found!"

"There was not enough left to give a positive match from the enzymes so I had a DNA extract from the flesh." He paused and looked sideways at Elect-Si.

"The gardener was one of Challis's wayward children. One that she has been hunting on and off for centuries."

Elect-Si added a second hand to massaging her full belly.

"Which one?"

"Enrico, The Younger."

"Does she know?"

"No. The last time I mentioned his name it was 1460. She cursed me for saying it and made me swear never to do so again. Also, she did not want to hear of his brother."

"Enrico, The Elder... I guess?"

Burkhardt smiled.

"Yes."

"What were their crimes?"

"They were fathered by the last Roman Governor in Palestine, just before the fall of the Empire in that part of the world. As they grew up, they fancied they had inherited Roman military genius. But they hadn't. Still, Challis gave them freedom to protect several thousand vampires ... an entire religious community migrating to Constantinople." Burkhardt sat back and cradled his coffee as he sipped from the oversized mug.

"There was a barbarian tribe sweeping through the area. There is evidence the brothers conspired with the Barbarians and let themselves be defeated. The migration was slaughtered."

"Did the Barbarians know those migrating were vampires?"

"No. They only wanted gold, silver, and jewels. There were many close friends of your mother in the migration."

"Fly … why not fly?"

"Possessions, babies, the old, and a few were sick." Burkhardt swirled his mug before continuing.

"After the massacre, the brothers showed off considerable wealth that came from the Barbarians. They were able to pay mercenary armies to carve out small empires of their own in Asia Minor."

XXXX

"And…"

"Challis erased the empires, but she never caught the brothers."

Elect-Si sat watching an eagle soaring on the thermals. So beautiful so relaxing to see how it managed its wings. She could feel her own wings itching to be spread and soar alongside the great bird of prey.

"The head had fangs." Burkhardt sipped at his coffee as he let the words sink in.

Elect-Si stared at Burkhardt as she continued to massage her pregnant belly.

"What are you looking at me like that for?" Asked Burkhardt.

"Get the doctor! My water just broke!" Said Elect-Si.

Canasta was walking with assurance and confidence; the bouncing step of her early strides was gone. Elect-Si mused on the fact that her daughter would soon need shoes. Canasta moved back and forth between the flowers hanging over the verandah railings and her new baby sister.

"Was I really that wrinkled and ugly when I was birthed?"

Elect-Si stared at Canasta. Those were words that came out of her daughters' mouth, they had not been placed in her mind telepathically.

Canasta turned and looked at her mother.

"I have been practising speaking with Brielle and Gwendoline. Now, tell me. Was I that ugly? Be honest."

"To a mother…"

"Cut the crap! Was I that ugly?"

"Yes, you were." Elect-Si smiled thinly as she gave her daughter an honest appraisal.

"Shit! But I guess I will grow up to be as beautiful as you." Canasta wandered into the suite and was gone.

Elect-Si tuned to her baby lying on the couch next to her and started adjusting the red crocheted blanket that kept the gentle breeze on the verandah from chilling her daughter.

As she did so, she was aware of someone coming and sitting on the chair across the coffee table from her. She looked up.

"Gwen, good morning, how are you?"

"Exhausted! Has Canasta told you, she has been practising speech with me? That little girl is so demanding so … so, exhausting. And I see you have another. How many are you and Manuel planning on having?"

"Well, if you will take on the role of Godmother to Canasta, you have to expect her to ask you for things." Elect-Si turned and looked at her baby. She and Manuel had never spoken about how many children they intended to have.

"We have not spoken about how many babies we will have." She looked up at Gwendoline.

"It will be a difficult conversation. I am immortal, he is not." Her voice trailed off.

Gwendoline put her hands together as if she were praying.

"I have a strong feeling it will go well when you have that discussion." Her gaze changed to the new baby.

"Have you thought of a name?"

"No … but I guess that is why you are here."

Gwendoline looked thoughtful, she closed her eyes for a moment and then opened them, still staring at the baby.
"You may not like it but just try…"

She turned her gaze to Elect-Si and stared at her with an intensity that gave her the feeling that she really did not have any choice.

"Ulaan sakhiusan tenger…"

"What the fuck does that mean?"

"Red Angel." Gwendoline put her hands in her lap.

"It is Mongolian. You can ask your mother, she encountered a White Shaman, who had red wings and always dressed in red. She was known in many tribes as the Red Angel. She was legendary for her treatment of Black Shaman who crossed her path, or the tribe she was with. She would literally incinerate them."

"And so … that is to be the name for my baby?"

"Ulaan will do when you want her to come and eat, or stop doing something she should not … she will be one mischievous child. Rather like her mother, before she became a vampire. You were a terribly naughty human child, weren't you?"

"I don't recall…" replied Elect-Si as she shrugged off the question.

Gwendoline, smiled broadly, and then broke into bright, sunny laughter. Slowly the laughter died away and she stood up and started to move towards the verandah door.

"Well, I thought I would mention it. Just an idea, a seed. Let the seed grow. Have you checked her finger nails, if not, Brielle can help? I think… I think you will find Ulaan can scratch."

Gwendoline stared at Elect-Si.

"Well, don't you want to know?"

"Know what?"

"If Ulaan is immortal, like you?"

"Is she?"

Gwendoline moved to the couch and looked over Elect-Si's shoulder at the baby. She reached down to stroke the babies unusually long, red hair.

"Ask Amunet." She leaned forward, placing a hand on Elect-Si's shoulder. Her face came close Elect-Si's ear.

"Nice red blanket … don't you think?" Then she was gone.

"Fuck! It's Cold!" exclaimed Elect-Si. The strong, relentlessly cold wind blew the snow into her face like so many small grains of sand. It seemed so hard that she had to hold her hand up to her face to stop the agony. Her hand was covered by a thick animal skin mitten and the cloak that covered and protected her was thick and dense. The thick fur collar that rested against her neck and face was warm and conforming to her body.

As she adjusted her seating position, she felt the thick wool trousers and animal skin boots she was wearing move against the dark granite on which she sat with surprising ease. She pulled the cloak more closely around herself and wondered at the idea of just pulling it over her head and lying there all wrapped up inside until the storm ended.

She bumped against someone or something. She pushed down the collar and looked at the flashing almond shaped eyes of Amunet set in her deeply tanned Egyptian skin.

"Invigorating, isn't it!" She exclaimed.

"Where the fuck is, we?" shouted Elect-Si above the howling wind.

Amunet grinned, her white teeth flashing against the blackness of the animal skin collar and the dark cloak she wore. From the corner of the cloak next to her refined chin, the arcing curve of a beautifully engraved Egyptian Khopesh framed her face. Her long black hair was held in place by gold hair rings decorated with lapis lazuli and rich symbols of Amunet's religious past. "I always come here when I want to feel the reality of the elements I control." She looked around as if the harsh blowing snow and ice were nothing to be concerned about.

"You are Egyptian. Could you not have chosen somewhere warm?"

"I appreciate all the elements, all the temperatures, and all the seasons everywhere. I have been here so many times over the centuries the locals know me, they invite me into their homes to eat, to sleep."

"Locals! I see no one through this storm." As her words disappeared into the wind, she heard Amunet chuckle.

Suddenly the wind died down, and was gone. Snow that had been falling horizontally, now drifted down peacefully.

"Is it that easy?"

"Yes." Amunet pointed the tip of her Khopesh in the direction of the now dimly seen far wall of rock. Clouds parted and a full moon illuminated the water several hundred feet below.

As her eyes adjusted Elect-Si could see the far wall suddenly fell down towards the water as of kneeling to it. Where it knelt there was land, broad, lush, and covered in trees and bushes, a river cut through the land and fell tumbling like a child over rocks and boulders in its river bed. Houses, with smoke drifting out of the smoke hole in the roof looked tranquil and interesting. The houses were each bounded by wooden railings that kept in a few animals, vegetable gardens, and small plantings of crops. Viking long ships rested sleepily at their moorings.

"Is that why we are here?" asked Elect-Si as her eyes glued to a ceremony being carried out on the wide shoreline.

"Partly. One of your ancestors."

A large tall cone of a wood burned brightly. Around the fire at a respectful distance, a large group of men, women and children were listening to the music and song of a small group of four men and two women. With the silence after the storm passing, the sound of the simple percussion and wind instruments seemed melodic and restful.

Around the fire a shaman danced. One hand filled with long white and black feathers from birds of prey, in the other, a staff topped with a jaw bone from a wolf or other predator. A long leather cloak, pants and boots decorated with sacred symbols painted with earth pigments. A polished metal Toli hung from animal sinew over his heart, another on his back, also over his heart so that a dark or evil spirit intending to do him harm could not attack the purity of his heart from either the front, or behind.

"One of my ancestors was a Viking shaman?"

"No silly. I meant a spiritual ancestor."

Suddenly the shaman darted towards the fire and from a bag he carried, he threw what looked like grain onto the fire. A moment later a huge plume of iridescent red sparks and flame shot skyward. As it did, he raised his arms and face to the sky and seemed to vibrate with energy. He cried out, not in pain, but to send a message to the Great Spirit above.

He reached into his bag and took out more grains and threw them on the fire. Another column of red fire and another cry. This was different. Then a third handful of grains and redder glowing, fiercely shimmering sparks and light.

"It is a ceremony, a song, a ritual for the souls of the dead who are being remembered. The shaman shouts out their names as he illuminates their path to the Great Spirit with the special red fire he creates."

"You have the souls?"

"Of course, I receive every soul of every man, woman and child. Every animal, every living thing. They are with me until they reincarnate into another life. The names he is calling out were a family that downed when their boat overturned in rough water." Amunet looked at Elect-Si.

"The daughter is over there by that woman in the white cloak. She has red hair. Her father called her a Red Angel. She is all that is left of that blood line."

"Red Angel ... like my baby."

"The soul that exists in your daughter, that also existed in that girl." She paused.

"Si, you are immortal. No one can do any harm to your physical body. Your Toli protects your soul, your soul can never be harmed. All souls are immortal. But that girl, her parents and brother and sister, they were human. Their body can die, but their soul continues on, reincarnation, over, and over again."

"So, we are here to watch and listen."

"No. Get up, we ... you, have work to do."

Elect-Si looked at where Amunet had been sitting and just saw the thick cloak, she looked up.

"I knew nothing could be easy!"

Amunet guided them on strong winds to a small clearing set amongst the dense forest of trees. Amunet brought her wickedly curved Khopesh into the moon light. It seemed to glow from the highly polished bronze. She looked at Elect-Si's quizzical expression.

"It's traditional engraved, it has traditional form but it was forged in Alexandria in this century." She looked at it admiringly.

"Titanium and tungsten with a carbide steel edge. Coated in bronze."

"But I guess there is a little secret source in it?"

"Oh yes. A very secret, and very powerful source."

Elect-Si felt something nudge against her side and opened her cloak. Her cane appeared from inside, the diamond handle glowing gently as it soaked up the full moonlight.

"What is that we have to do here?"

"Well, for starters, something you seem to like doing, giving a Black Shaman a dose of reality. For me, a little something I enjoy too."

Amunet and Elect-Si approached the ceremony from the gravelly beach that was the space between the land and the community and the waters that had claimed the lives of those big remembered. As they appeared from out of the blackness into the warm glow of the large fire, the attention shifted from the shaman to the newcomers.

The elder raised his hand and the ceremony stopped.

"You are welcome, angel from the east, you bring someone with you."

Amunet moved forward to be close to the fire.

"A powerful shaman to bless this ceremony and bless the Red Angel that still lives."

"The Red Angel is to be married to the leader of the Dark Wind hunters. She will be used in the ceremonies of their black shaman. It will bring them power and strength to do what they do in protecting us from all that would hurt our community."

Elect-Si felt something stir in her, it started to glow brightly. She looked down at it and felt Emma speak into her mind one word, "No."

Elect-Si moved forward to stand beside Amunet.

"The Red Angel will not leave this community." She was surprised at her voice, it seemed to be everywhere, rebounding off the rock walls and completely hiding the sound of the river, and the crackling of the fire.

The elder looked in the direction of his shaman and pointed to Elect-Si.

The Shaman nodded confidently and placed his staff in front of his face and looked through its teeth in Elect-Si's direction. After a moment the staff started to vibrate and shake violently. The jaw bone started to shine and then crumbled on to the ground. The shaman screamed and jumped back from the remains of the bone.

He stared at Elect-Si for several minutes as the gathering watched and waited, they had never seen two shamans in this strange battle for dominance.

Couching low behind the fire so that he could not be seen, he started to shake a bone rattle. After another few minutes, he slowly worked his way around it to take Elect-Si by surprise. At the last moment, he ran up to her violently shaking his rattle and issuing curses and casting spells.

Elect-Si raised her cane. She slowly raised the tip off the ground and with the tip, went the shaman until he was several feet off the ground, his legs, and feet kicking in the still air. All eyes in the community looked up in wonder, some had their hands over their eyes, shielding them from seeing what was happening. Others gasped as Elect-Si moved the tip of her cane close to the fire. The Shaman struggled but could not change what was happening. The tip of her cane drifted closer to the fire carrying the shaman with it.

Elect-Si looked past the fire at the elder.

"Do you want him back, or shall I burn him?"

Hearing her words, the shaman started shouting and gesturing at Elect-Si as he cast more spells in her direction.

"Give him back to me," said the elder after several minutes considering the panic in his shaman's expression.

"He is not a good shaman, he is not as powerful as you, but we like him."

Elect-Si moved the tip towards the elder and set the shaman down abruptly, the shaman stumbled, and fell on his hands and knees muttering as he did.

The sound of hooves on the rocky track beside the river made all turn and look in the direction of several riders approaching at a light canter.

The padded shoulders of the cloaks made the riders appear bigger than Elect-Si knew they were. In her mind, she heard Emma.

"The black shaman who cut off my arm. His spirit is in the one who rides with them."

The crowd moved apart to allow the rider's space but several were knocked over and almost trampled by the horses as the riders cared little for those who fell.

The riders drew into the circle and eyed the crowd. The leader of the group sat on his horse, looking around the gathering, until his eyes landed on the elder. He spat in the direction of the shaman on the ground.

"Such a weakling! Why do you put up with him?" He held out a hand to the rider next to him.

"We have an excellent shaman, a black one, one who travels with and speaks to the dark spirits of power and energy."

He dismounted and walked up to the elder. As he did, he stepped on the back of the shaman, and spat on him.

"Why waste time on this piece of shit? You could have so much more power if you only changed."

He slapped the elder's face.

"I am powerful. I take what I want. I think we will take a few of your young boys. There is need for them in the brothels." He looked around the crowd until his eyes settled on a girl of about 11 with red hair.

"I have come for the Red Angel."

"I want that one, the one with the bent sword and the dark eyes, the tanned skin. I think she will be a good slave."

Another rider was dismounting and moving towards Amunet.

"Perhaps I will let her play with her sword, a few passes with good and then I will have her." He gestured to a space on the ground by the fire.

"Then, I will have her here." As he moved, he drew his sword and took a violent, lunging swing at her. She parried it easily which caused great laughter amongst the other riders. One did not laugh. The black shaman's eyes were locked on Elect-Si.

The rider held his sword high above his head.

"This is good steel, Ulfberht steel, from Germania. One more pass and either I will split apart your legs or this will, you have a choice." He came at Amunet again, this time with a blow from a high guard position.

Amunet did not move, her feet stayed grounded but the Khopesh glittered in a bronze-coloured arc in the light from the fire, and the clear, bright moon. The rider's sword shattered, and fell in pieces from contact with her unique sword.

A loud grunt of surprise came from the rider as he looked at his prized possession which now lay broken on the ground. He let go of the handle and it rattled on the fragments, and a small rock.

Behind him the sound of snickering and laughter broke out from several other riders.

"Perhaps she will do the same for your cock!" Shouted one.

"I said that was a bad blade. You never went to Germania, you bought it from a sailor in the back room of a whore house in Sweden, and you were drunk."

The rider turned around to look at his tormenters.

"That was the sword I bested you with, twice, and I killed that elder several fjords north of here when he decided to fight me. It was a good sword; it was truly from Ulfberht. Now she will pay!"

The rider shrugged off his cloak and pulled out a dagger as he did.

His face contorted in anger, the rider moved surprisingly quickly towards Amunet, for a second, she appeared rooted to the spot and then moved sideways, avoiding his lung and bringing the Khopesh around in an arcing curve. The Egyptian sword glittered again as it separated the rider's head from his body. The head spun in the air as it flew towards the fire. Amunet pushed over the still standing corpse.

As she also removed her cloak, her fire dragon sat on her shoulder for a long moment. Gasps could be heard all around the fire. Dragons are an ethereal being, they live with the Gods, they breathe fire and flame to cleanse the earth. A fire that cleaned out dead wood from a forest was started by a dragon so that only good trees could grow for its nest.

Dragons stood proudly at the head of Viking long boats to light the way and see in the dark, when the boats pulled up onto the shore of a foreign land, it was a dragon that looked for a safe to land.

It flapped its wings several times as its eyes narrowed and focused on the riders. Amunet reached up and stroked its belly, it lent its head close to hers so that she could whisper in its ear. It straightened up and its wings beat with explosive energy and it shot forward with lightning speed at the riders. Breathing fire, its claws out stretched, hungry for flesh, its first breath of dragon fire engulfed a rider to the right. His horse panicked and threw the burning rider to the ground.

Hovering above the burning prey the fire dragon breathed more fire and suddenly the screaming stopped and the rider lay motionless. The smell of burning flesh started to waft around the gathering.

A rider behind the fore dragon drew his sword as he tried to control his panicking horse. The Fire Dragon easily rotated in midair and exhaled a ball of intense fire at the rider. It landed squarely on his chest and ran up into his face and open mouth. He dropped his sword as he grappled with the reins of his horse and the fire engulfing his body. A second ball of fire erupted from the dragon's mouth and knocked the rider from his saddle but a foot caught in the stirrup.

The horse dragged the burning body behind it as it struggled up the track they had just descended.

An arrow cut through the air towards the dragon.

A blazing wall of flame shot from the Fire Dragon's mouth and consumed the arrow. It fell harmlessly in burning fragments to the ground.

The dragon's head turned to the direction of the rider who fired it. Its red eyes glowed fiercely, its head dropped slightly and the wings beat viciously to give it a tremendous attack. As it skimmed over the head of the rider, the dragon's mighty talons buried themselves into his face. He screamed. The wings beat harder, and he was lifted his horse and carried towards the bonfire.

Screaming and struggling violently, part of the side of his face tore aware from his head, embedded on the talons. The Fire Dragon's wings propelled them forward and at the right moment. The talons released and the rider fell into the fire where he struggled and screamed with his burning clothing and searing flesh.

He rolled out on to the ground, all his clothing on fire. Somehow, he managed to shed his cloak which showed his back was smoking, but not on fire. He patted at his burning hair with his hands as he screamed louder and louder.

The Fire Dragon hovered over him like an avenging angel and breathed more fire down onto his back setting all of him alight.

His motions, slowed, his screaming became less intense. He slumped to his knees, fiery head staring out at the boats and the fjord. Slowly his head bent forward, chin resting on his chest, the fire consumed him like a small version of the bonfire that now burned brightly behind him.

"I will have both of you whores screaming as the skin is stripped from your bodies," bellowed the leader as he started to unsheathe his sword and dismount.

"Wait!" shouted the shaman rider.

"That one is mine." He pointed at Elect-Si.

The leader stopped and looked where the shaman was pointing.

"You have business with her, you know her?"

"From a past life." He removed his cloak and pulled his shaman's staff from its place on his saddle.

"I cut an arm from a girl to celebrate a demon I was speaking to. The demon had me curse the girl so that anyone who tried to grow the arm back would themselves be cursed. Many tried, all failed, some would not even attempt it because of the curse." He adjusted the metal Toli over his heart.

"She grew back the arm … she ignored the curse. I must … bring fire and curses down on her."

"Do what you must, shaman. Then, I will burn her. For now, I will take the other." He moved away from his horse towards Amunet.

Elect-Si waited; Emma vibrated her Shaman's staff in excitement. She shrugged her shoulders and stepped out from under her cloak. The cloak stood there, in the air, unsupported. Elect-Si simply needed to walk back into its shape and wear it. The crowd looked on in amazement.

She could now see her warm boots and thick woollen trousers that protected her legs. She wore a fine leather bouse with elegant leather cords that tied it closed at the neck and wrists. Elect-Si started to smile, her nipples rubbed against the inside of the leather blouse as she moved, she felt them start to stiffen.

Her attention returned to the Black Shaman walking towards her. He was shouting curses and spells.

For the first time, Elect-Si felt them. They were like small, delicate summer raindrops falling from a sudden and unexpected shower, they rolled off her and were gone.

The shaman stopped and glared at her.

"You wear no Toli, your heart will burn and shrivel up. You will beg for life, so that I can take it from you… I will do it over, and over again." As he spoke, he thrust his Shaman's staff forward in Elect-Si direction. He bellowed more curses and spells.

"I wear no Toli, because I am my Toli. Look deeper, be at one with your demons, talk to them. You will find they fear me. You say you are a Black Shaman, be open to the blackness in me. Look at the whiteness in me."

The Black Shaman pulled a rattle from his belt and started to wave it, and make noise with it in Elect-Si's direction. He threw back his head and bellowed at the clear star laden sky. The bellow formed words and a song. He beat his chest. He shook his staff at the sky. Slowly, close to the Milky Way galaxy that ripped across the cloudless sky like a wound, a tear started to his left. A sinkhole began, small at first but widening.

In her mind, Elect-Si heard Emma.

"This is how it started before, when he cut off my arm. Demons fell from the sky and came out of the earth."

"Does it go on for long, this is boring?" Elect-Si looked around as. Amunet had dispatched the leader already. Elect-Si thought it would have been interesting to watch what had happened as the leader was lying on the ground with his own sword in his mouth. A good third of it sticking out from the back of his head.

Elect-Si turned her attention back to the Black Shaman. From the sink hole, several small what appeared to be monkeys appeared. Only they were unlike any you would see in a zoo, or on TV.

They had no fur, they were naked, their skin was black and there was no skin or muscle on their face that she could see. The head was skeletal bone. Their eyes, seemed to swivel on stalks, as intense, round, lollipops. Their fingers grew slender and narrow, ending with long sharp nails that could pick small magots from a decaying corpse to feast on.

From a rip the sky, black birds circled and then slowly fluttered down. As they landed, they grew and became terrifying vultures and birds of prey. They were the size of a man. Talons and beaks ready to rip flesh from bone and a spirit from the flesh.

The circle of villagers cowered but was rooted to the spot in fascination of what would happen next.

The black shaman looked at what he had conjured and seemed pleased with them.

"She is yours, do what you will, but do it so we can all see." He looked at Elect-Si from the corner of his eye.

"Then take the souls of all these villagers for your pleasure and their pain."

The monkeys looked at Elect-Si but did not move. The vultures fluttered their wings and started to groom their feathers again. Finally, one of the monkeys looked at the shaman.

"No."

The black shaman pointed his staff directly at Elect-Si.

"I order you."

"You cannot order us to do something we cannot do." The monkey stared at Elect-Si.

"She is both the black and white from before all existed. Before there was life in the universe."

"She wears no Toli for protection against you. Do what you do worse."

The monkey turned fully towards Elect-Si.

"She wears no Toli because her being is Toli. The original Toli." The monkey slowly covered his face with his deformed hands, and bowed to Elect-Si. The action was followed by the other monkeys.

One by one, the vultures turned towards Elect-Si and brought their large wings up and covered their heads and faces for several minutes. As they brought their wings down, all but one flapped them vigorously and started to take flight and fly up to the rip in the sky.

The black shaman stood opened mouthed looking at the birds fly away.

"She healed the girl whose arm you cut off because she could. Your spells and curses mean nothing to her. They are like the final drips of piss from a cock that has just urinated."

Some of the monkeys were starting to turn to the sink hole one took hold of the arm of the speaker, pulling it towards the hole but he shrugged it off. He looked from Elect-Si to the Black Shaman.

"We do your bidding because you cast a spell over us. Make your peace with life because she has business with you that will end it." The monkey turned to Elect-Si and again covered its face and bowed to her. It slipped back towards the hole but did not get in. It stood watching, waiting. For a moment it looked over at the remaining vulture, each nodded at the other.

The black Shaman turned towards Elect-Si and stumbled back a step when he found she was now only arm's length away. An expression of terror on his face.

Elect-Si lifted her cane and its gold tip touched his staff. Instantly as it made contact, the staff burst into fire. The shaman screamed, he tried to let go of the staff, to let it fall to the ground, but his hand seemed unable to open its fingers, he screamed loudly, as Elect-Si reached into the fire and held his hand more tightly to the now towering flames. Pressing him to the cleansing fire.

"There is a soul in the staff whom you have imprisoned and tortured for all of your life. In this moment, I am free that soul." The flames abruptly stopped, the smoking staff started to flake ash and from the top a white wispy smoke appeared.

The smoke played in the air, it spiralled upwards and then spread out as if enjoying the freedom from the confinement of the staff. It formed a ball in front of Elect-Si for a moment and then started to slowly spin as it moved to Amunet and disappeared into the palm of her outstretched hand.

Elect-Si moved the tip of her cane until it was in front of the shaman's face. His eyes focused on the shiny gold that gave him a strange reflection of himself.

He started to scream. It was a scream that breaks vocal cords, shreds them like pulled pork.

Elect-Si squeezed her grip on his burned limb and he burst into flame. His body was a column of fire. He screamed and struggled against her grip. As they stood there, his clothes fell away, skin was consumed, his eyes were burned out and the flush on his cheeks disappeared.

As soon as she had started the fire, Elect-Si stopped it.

"I want your soul. I want it now!"

A thicker wispy smoke started to flow out of the standing, burned corpse. It started to form a shape but, in the end, it hung there limply.

"All of it… I want all of you…" hissed Elect-Si.

The fames started again from her hand and spread all over the charred corpse. The flames became a roar that sent a column of fire high into the sky. As the height of the tower grew so did the intensity.

"All of it… I want all of you…" hissed Elect-Si again with much more force, and venom in her voice.

In the sink hole, the monkeys came back to watch in wonderment at the brightness of the column of fire.

As the column slowly grew less and less, the brightness died away and the bare skeleton of the black shaman stood for a moment, and then collapsed. A ball of smoke hovered in the air, drawing in the other white smoke that hung in the air.

Elect-Si opened her hand and let go of any remaining fragments of the staff and the dead shaman's fingers.

Suddenly, her hand darted towards the ball of wispy smoke and it seemed to writhe as one complete being. Tendrils of smoke wrapped around her wrist, but then shot away from her as her existence, her Toli, made itself known.

The diamond handle of her cane started to glow brightly, the colour of pure sunlight. The intensity grew and grew until the bonfire was a fraction of the light that illuminated the villagers, the village, the vulture, and monkeys. The vulture turned away from the light and the monkeys looked at the ground.

Elect-Si brought the tip over, down, onto and then into the ball of wispy smoke. It struggled vigorously against her grip but Elect-Si continued to press the cane's tip into the ball which glowed from the inside out with pure white light.

Like a red-hot ball of metal, a branding iron, pressed into a slave's back, she pressed harder, and deeper.

The entire ball began to glow white and pure, the tendrils now limp grew white, and clean, and pure.

Elect-Si slowly took the gold tip out of the smoke and looked at the ball now limp, purified.

Elect-Si felt Amunet's hand on her arm. She turned to look into the dark almond shaped eyes and smiling lips.

"I'll take that. It's mine to deal with now."

She watched as Amunet reached out and touched the ball of smoke, it disappeared into her palm.

"You will not hurt us?" the voice was quiet, hesitant.

The words came from the monkey now sitting on the edge of the sink hole. The vulture stood close by, listening intently to what was said.

"Go back to where you came from. Do not cross my path or give me reason to think of you again."

As the monkey turned to the sink hole, he looked back over his shoulder.

"He put a spell on us, he called us, we had to obey. We could do nothing else." He slipped into the hole which closed after him. As he did so, the vulture took flight and soared towards the closing rip in the sky.

Across the dying bonfire Elect-Si could make out the red-haired girl, the Red Angel. She smiled at the girl. With surprising assurance, the girl raised her hand and waved at Elect-Si, then a broad smile spreads across her young face. A comforting mother's hand came over her shoulder to make sure the cape the girl was wearing continued to keep the girl warm.

The mother's cape slipped from her face for a moment as she stands tall. Her eyes meet Elect-Si's.

"Mother! Is that you?" Elect-Si muttered. How could her mother be here, now, watching? She opened her mouth to speak louder, forcefully. But the villagers are moving forward, cheering, they press their offerings of gratitude. The Red Angel and the woman with her... Mother... Challis... Chi.

Are gone.

Elect-Si kissed the glowing diamond handle of her cane in the confusion, and felt Emma's peace giving vibrations.

Sequins. A sequined silhouette. All Channel, Lagerfeld, and Louis V. Hair drifting on the gentle spring night air, street lights that glow less brightly than they should. Loose breasts moving under silk. The clip-clip of elegant sandals as the wearer moves quickly from shadow to shadow. Pausing for a moment under a street lamp to glance into a purse. To pull out a gold-framed mirror and stare into its silvery reflection to check hair, and lip gloss.

The sound of a screen door rattling on a service entrance behind a high mansion wall. The hushed sounds of a woman and a man.

Silence.

Then grunting, moaning. The creaking of a garden table, and sounds of frantic fucking.

She puts the mirror away and closes the purse clasp with certainty and stares at the road ahead and holds the purse close to her body. She takes a moment to look at her Cartier Tank watch and sets a determined expression on her perfect lips.

Now.

To walk briskly on, not run. A hand pressed to her chest, as if to slow the speed of her heart.

Disappearing around a corner onto a side street, a corner half hidden by an overgrown weeping willow. Pushing the tears of the willow away, as it is hoped the tears of life will be pushed away, she continues.
Pausing under another street lamp. Opening the purse and taking out the gold mirror to check that the willow did not displace her perfect hair. Nothing is out of place.

Checking the lipstick preparing for a kiss.

A black Mercedes pulls up by the street lamp and the driver emerges, he nods to the woman and a flash of white teeth glow for a moment in the light of the lamp. He takes a small step in her direction. Holds out a hand.

The woman smiles back and takes a small step towards the driver.

She stops.

She looks down into her purse, as if looking for something.

She finds what she is looking for.

She takes out a pistol, with a silencer.

She points it at the driver's head and pulls the trigger.

Once.

Twice.

A bullet through each eye…

Bone, blood, and brains explode from the back of the driver's head, landing on the roof of the Mercedes. They make the sound of heavy Mediterranean rain landing on the roof when the car is driven at speed along the coast road, from Monaco to Nice.

The driver's legs crumple and he slumps, slumps against the side of the car.

Small puffs of smoke hung in the air.

The pistol is carefully put away and the woman moves towards an arm caught by the wing mirror and turns it over. She pushes back the crisp white Egyptian cotton cuff and its gold cuff link. The heart is still pumping, she senses the pressure of blood in the veins. Like the perfect predator she is, she bites down on them.

She feeds.

As she stands, the gold mirror appears, she uses the light of the street lamp to check her hair and smudged lip gloss. She licks blood from her lips.

She reaches into the purse and takes out an applicator and brings it up to her lips and applies gloss to complete her perfection.

She puts the mirror away and closes the purse clasp with conviction and stares at the road ahead. She reaches down and slips off her sandals and clasps them, and her purse, close to her body, and sets a determined expression on her lips … her chin.

On bare feet, she moves silently down the street.
She moves silently into darkness.

The bathroom was palatial. A large white enamel soaker tub stood a few feet back from the floor to ceiling windows through which early morning sunlight warmed the white tiles and glinted off the highly polished brass and copper tub fittings. Large white, plush towels warmed themselves in the sun.

Pope Sophyra gripped the edge of the tub as she leaned over coughing violently. Blood splatters covered the bottom of the tub. As she stood up, inhaling a lungful of air, she caught sight of herself in the mirror. Blood covered her chin and lips; it ran down her neck and between her breasts. She ran her fingers in the red liquid, smearing it more widely across her breasts. She brought her fingers up to examine her blood.

Then, she remembered her breath, and leaned down to gather the handle on the edge of the tub and coughed a huge violent stream of air, noise and blood into the tub. The blood on her hands made it difficult to hold on to the top and she struggled not to fall onto the hard metal tub.

The doctor turned away from monitor and looked at Lady Challis and Elect-Si.

"That has been going on almost daily for an hour or more since we removed the enzyme glands. And. Look at the blood on her thighs. On the floor. She menstruates heavily when she tries spitting her enzymes. We have had to keep her naked so we can clean her up easily. She will pass out in a few minutes."

"I am not sure I care that much," muttered Elect-Si.
"She has to return to being Pope Sophyra." Said Lady Challis turning to her daughter.

"You control her. What do you want done?"

Elect-Si looked at the challenging stare she was receiving.

"I think you already know that." She turned to look at the screen and Pope Sophyra slowly slid down the side of the tub and sprawled unconscious on the floor.

"A truly sterile Pope would have its advantages…." She turned to the doctor.

"Get it done. Womb, ovaries, take it all. If there is any research, anything we can learn from them. All the better."

On the monitor, white-suited orderlies moved into the bathroom and placed the unconscious Pope onto a gurney and prepared to wheel it away.

"Now, do it now!" She turned to her mother.

"Test her blood, test the blood in the tub. Look for anything out of the ordinary. Especially. Enzymes." Commanded Lady Challis.

"What is that for?" Asked Elect-Si aggressively.

"Oh, something a child told me before he went to sleep."

Elect-Si needed some peace. Some quiet. Some time to rest. Some time to clear her mind. She drew her knees up under her chin and rested her head on them. She closed her eyes and listened to the wind as it meandered peacefully through the canyons and gorges of the Himalayas. She had flown quietly through several of them tonight and smelled the scent of fires. They burned in secret, behind rocks and boulders, giving away their presence as little as possible. There were far more Yeti here than anyone had imagined. It was oddly restful watching them, seeing how they cared for each other, especially the young.

Two nights ago, she had the honour to watch a Yeti die and be buried. Oddly, there were no lamentations, no wailing, no message from those still living to the gods to look after the soul of the one who had died. Just the matter of fact moving of the body to a sheltered, spot where it could be broken by pummelling with boulders.

She wondered for a moment why that was, then she realized that a broken and bleeding body would decay faster. Attract predators to devour it. Last night she had followed a solemn group higher up the canyon. The journey had taken her to a place where the bleaching bones of several yetis lay exposed. Tufts of fur lay all around.

Methodically and carefully, the group took each bone and with a rock, broke, and ground it to small fragments. Last was the skull. The group must have known the owner of the skull when he or she was living. They venerated the skull and splashed it with oils, probably made from plants but she could not tell from her perch.

She realized she was watching the reason why humans had never found Yeti skeletons. The group, the tribe managed the body in such a way that little evidence of it would be found. She had a fleeting thought that all of this effort was only because of humans. Humans searching for the sacred and special beings. Their intention to capture and take one away to experiment on and study with no regard for the Yeti family.

It made her sad. Very sad. It made her feel she had a duty to protect the special creatures. She brought her cane close to her, and reached out in her thoughts to the soul in the cane, Emma. What would you do, say, she wondered?

Suddenly, she felt something solid and special at her back. It was the tree of life, Ash Yggdrasil. Close to her hands were a collection of different fruits, bounty from the great canopy of abundance above her.

Outside of the laden tree, the sky was alight with the amber and orange glow of sunset. Away in the distance the village Emma had promised to show her one day was slipping into the warm glow of night fires, candles and cooking fires.

Emma appeared from behind the tree.

"I have been picking some of the fruits you like the most." She lay them down on the ground next to Elect-Si.

"Thank you." Murmured Elect-Si as she picked up one of the oranges and started to peel and eat it. The taste of the fruit always seemed so more intense and purer in the upper world. It exploded into her mouth and she struggled to keep all the juice on and swallow it.

Emma sat down on a gnarled root and looked at Elect-Si.

"You can't save them, not all of them. The Yeti, you cannot save what is not supposed to exist."

Elect-Si stared at Emma.

"Is that true? They are not supposed to exist."

"The Yeti is special beings, as are like the Banjhakri whom you speak to, and learn from. They are from a time when for them to exist was right and proper. There was a balance between them, nature, and humans. But the balance with humans has been lost. Mankind's insatiable curiosity and ability to craft tools and seek out knowledge, to understand, and to use what they learn is not tempered with the need to leave things as they are."

Suddenly, Emma smiled and her eyes glittered as she looked at Elect-Si.

"You have the ability to move through time, you could go back to the moment when the balance was upset and study it. See it for what it was."

" … and change it?"

"No! You cannot change what happened."

"But I stopped Hades from coming into the present or the future."

"That was different. That was a person, the spirit of a soul trying to break out of their place in time and change the present so that they could exist in the future."

"I helped Amunet destroy Amun. Is that the same thing?"

"Yes. Exactly. The essence of Amun is where it should be in time and place."

Elect-Si started eating from a small pile of strawberries, Emma had set out for her.

"So, the Yeti, they will die out eventually?"

"No, they will always be with you, humans, and myself. But only special people such as us will see them." Emma straightened her dress.

"You will always protect them." She looked up at Elect-Si.

"As you watch them, so they watch you. You know that, don't you? They let you watch them because they know you are different from humans. They watch you fly."

Elect-Si stared at Emma.

"They have been watching me when I go to the mountains?"

"Yes. From the first time, they chased you. They have been watching you. When you are walking up in the canyons, or flying overhead."

"I never knew!"

"All the spirits and souls that wish to live outside of their time. You are the Gatekeeper, they want to know where you are and what you are doing, and they watch for any possibility to get past the gate."

"I only thought of Hades and Amun. How many more are there?"

"How many clouds are there in the sky, how many grains of sand on a beach?" Emma frowned.

"I know that sounds whimsical, but … it is not just the Gods that want to exist outside their time. It could be a parent who died before their child grew to adulthood and wants to come back and protect the child who is now an adult, and in danger. How many parents died while their son or daughter was away at war. How many soldiers made a bond to protect each other, and then one is killed?"

Emma picked a blade of long grass and pressed it between her thumbs and blew through the gap. The blade resonated like the reed in an instrument and created a complex but eerie sound.

"I guess I will know when they try to cross the gate. At whatever level they are?"

"Yes. The gate is like this blade of grass, it will vibrate, and you will be called. You will judge. You will enforce."

"Forever?"

"Forever sounds as if it has an ending. There is no ending for you, or for me, as I will always be with you. There is no finite, there is infinity. Time will end and you will look back on it, and carry on."
"I have heard that said many times, what does it mean? What is there after time?"

"Think of time as being a cycle of existence. As one cycle ends, so another will start from that ending." Emma paused to see how her words were being received. If she needs to provide more clarification.

"There have been endless cycles before this one and there will be endless ones after it. Humans see time as linear, but really it is cyclical. The next cycle will be everything that in this existence has not, could not be considered, or, cannot be comprehended. You are resting against the tree of life, Ash Yggdrasil. That tree has seen endless cycles."

"You make it sound tiring?"

Emma giggled.

"I thought you would say that!"

Elect-Si reached down for another strawberry, but her hand felt meat, cooked meat. She looked down in surprise, there was a piece of cooked meat which had some herbs rubbed on it and a few berries.

"The Yeti left that for you. A token of their respect and to help you understand they know and that they are not a danger to you.

Eat! They are watching and they want you to know their gift is acceptable."

"They were here!" Exclaimed Elect-Si, stunned by the fact she had not been aware of their visit. How could she have not been aware of such a large creature being close enough to leave food for her?

"Eat!" repeated Amunet.

Elect-Si slowly picked up the meat. It was well cooked and the herbs were tasty. She ate hungrily. The berries provided a juicy counterpoint to the taste of the meat. As she looked up, she saw Amunet was sitting like an elf on a nearby boulder.

"It will be the sun rise soon, and you need to be back at the palace."

" … and there is a convenient, powerful, jet stream that will get me there supper fast!"

"Yes."

Lady Challis walked slowly and at peace through her gardens at the palace. The beautiful flowers and the rich scent they gave off were intoxicating, the colours a treasure for the eyes. She stopped to sit on a marble bench and simply just watch the flowers as they moved back and forth in the gentle breeze.

Immortality had brought many such moments. She treasured them and remembered them all. She turned her right palm skyward and, in her mind, the shinning head waters of the River Nile passed across it. She was contemplating a dugout canoe, some possessions and a little food and well water. This was the moment she set out to follow the Nile which would eventually, across a couple of centuries bring her to Egypt and Narmer. Beside the canoe were some beautiful flowers and she picked a few, just a few, to put into the canoe as a remembrance of where she had come from.

As she turned her other hand over, the palm revealed a cluster of rather scrubby flowers and a small bush. Set amongst the unending blue skies of Tengri and the green grass of the steppes, these flowers were a riot of uncontrolled colour. She had camped there for a few days as she rested, letting her horse regain its energy after days of hard riding. It had fed on the long deep rich grass and drank from a gurgling stream.

She closed each hand in turn and the memories faded, her horse remained for a few moments longer, looking at her wistfully, she thought.

The sound of footsteps on the gravel path made her look up. The steps were too light and brisk for whom she expected. They were not Brielle's steps, nor were they, her daughter's.

Gwendoline appeared, smiling, her pale features and white hair contrasting with a grey and black sari. Over her head, shielding her from the sun she twirled an umbrella.

"Well, Sister, have you decided?"

"That umbrella, a little large, isn't it?"

"It is what they call a Golfing Umbrella. The last thing the Goddess of the North can do is return to her people with a suntan. This will keep the sun off me."

"Maybe you should get a suntan. It would be good for you. Do something … be something different for once."

Gwendoline frowned.

"Sister, different, has always been your domain. I prefer to keep it simple and always be what I was born to be."

"Well. Have you decided?"

"No!"

"Oh, this is going to be one of those role-playing games."

Gwendoline sat down on a small bench slightly at an angle from her sister.

"Do you think he knows?"

"I am not sure."

Lady Challis's mind slid easily into the memory of a small boy, barefoot, dressed in rags and cowering in a corner. His bones showing through his skin almost everywhere. Her men picked the vainly struggling boy up and carried him off to a safe place where he could be healed, fed, and educated.

"It was the inquisition. Sweeping out of Spain into France. His parents had been murdered by the town's folk. He hid and ran from the dogs the human let chases him for sport. There was no evidence his parents were vampires or that he was. They just knew he was different and they destroyed anyone or anything that was different," Lady Challis frowned. Difficult times. That is how we met."

"Hmmm and you are telling me to be different and get a suntan. Do you wish to try and kill me? You can't you know that, don't you?" Gwendoline twirled the umbrella.

"You have slept with him so many times over the centuries, and you never noticed?"

"So have you, and you never noticed either?" Asked Lady Challis.

The sound of heavier, masculine footsteps on the gravel brought silence and their attention to who turned the corner next.

"M'lady. Gwendoline. It is good to see you both."

Lady Challis patted the space on the marble bench next to her.

"I have something to talk about and you are the only one who can help."

Burkhardt sat down next to her. He clasped his hands together as he looked at Gwendoline. Then he half turned to look at Lady Challis.

"How can I help?"

"When I found you, your parents had been murdered, why was that?"

Burkhardt stared down at his hands, which began to fidget.

"They were different, and so was I. That is why they set the dogs on me whenever I showed my face. My parents were too old to run. They were killed. Stabbed and hacked to death." He paused as the wave of emotion passed through his features.

"I watched their bodies being burned, from high up in a tree. The priest. The bloody priest! He said they were killed for being different but even he did not know how different."

He paused and looked out at the flowers and the greenery.

"One time when the dogs were chasing me, I could run no further… I was exhausted. One of the dogs was going for my throat… I put my hands up and the palm, this one…" he held up is right hand.

"It touched the dog's nose as I pushed it away. I wanted the dog to die so badly." Burkhardt sat back into the benches' backrest.

"I watched the dog crawl away and die. But they still caught me. They put me in a cage on a small cart along with some other boys they had caught. They took us to a castle where a lord looked us over. One of the boys who was a bit fatter than the rest of us was dragged out and roped over a barrel and stripped. I thought he was going to be flogged or canned." Burkhardt closed his eyes and paused. Breathing heavily, he opened his eyes.

"The soldiers raped him over and over until blood was running down his legs from his anus. Then they cut his throat and dragged his body away to a large cook fire. Then they left."

Silence.

Burkhardt looked around at Lady Challis and Gwendoline.

"Just before dawn a soldier came to the cage and dragged me out. He took behind the stables. He said I would get the same as the other boy unless I gave myself to him. When I did not know what to say, he took me by the hair into one of the stalls… I knew what would happen and held onto his wrist and wished for him to die, like the dog had." Burkhardt coughed to clear his throat.

"He staggered back against the wall and slowly slid down to the floor and just sat there. His mouth was moving, but no sound came out. Then his mouth stopped moving and I knew he was dead. I ran. Oh, did I run? So fast and for so long ... so long, my heart pounded and my eyes seemed to fill with blood."

"Did anything else happen when you held on to people?" Asked Gwendoline.

"There was a farmer. I worked like a slave on his farm for a few months. It was not bad really, I had food and a corner of the stables. One day he took some pigs to market and came home with a bottle of liquor and got drunk. He came into the stables looking for me. He wanted the same as the soldier. He was holding me down but I managed to get hold of his ankle and ... he died."

"My men took hold of you when they found you..."

"Why did they not die? M'lady. You appeared so beautiful, looking down at me from your stallion. The men had hold of me, yes, but they did not grip me with evil intent. I could sense the difference and felt nothing bad would happen to me." He turned to Lady Challis, and smiled. Nothing has. I thank you for that."

"You have fangs... I have felt them in your mouth ... with my tongue."

Burkhardt slowly opened his mouth and at the right moment, small fangs extended. He held his mouth open for a few seconds and then closed it.

"They are much smaller than yours... I never have the desire to bite anyone or anything. When I want them dead, I try to touch them." He looked down at his open hands and then rubbed them together. In the sunlight a sheen appeared on his palms and fingers. It glittered in the sunlight and then disappeared into his skin.

"Pope Sophyra. We found some enzymes in her blood. Are they yours?"

Burkhardt leaned back and looked at the sky… "Momma, Papa … please help me!" He turned to Lady Challis.

"I think so. I was helping the orderly one morning. She was cursing and said something that sounded like words the priest had used when defiling my parents. All of a sudden, I was back in the tree watching his ugly mouth spewing those disgusting words that he said were in the Bible…. I wanted her to die a terrible death. Not a quick one. A terrible. Terrible. Death." He paused and took several deep breaths.

"An orderly interrupted my thoughts and I lost my grip on her. She probably did not receive all that I intended her to get." He waited for a few moments.

"Will she die?"

Lady Challis stared into Burkhardt's eyes.

"No. All the bloodletting is purging your enzymes. She should be alright today."

Burkhardt looked deflated, sad, lost.

"I cannot say I wish her well. But I am glad she is not going to die. At least not the way I wished her to." He coughed nervously.

"What will happen to me?"

Lady Challis slowly stood, straightened her sari and cast a glance at Gwendoline. She turned to Burkhardt.

"I need a strong Head Butler. You are that person. Stand tall, strong, and take my arm, I need you to walk with me through the gardens. I need you to show me the new blooms. I need to understand more about your species. You are the fourth variation we have encountered." Her face took on a serious expression.

"On no account must you tell Sophyra about yourself, what you are, or what happened? Let's keep those our little secrets." She turned to Gwendoline.

"Isn't that, right?"

As Burkhardt gazed up at Lady Challis, he slowly smiled, and got to his feet. He pulled himself up to his full height and straightened his shirt over his now proud chest. He reached out to give Lady Challis his arm. They turned to look at Gwendoline who was now rising from her seat and putting down her umbrella.

"I will walk back to the palace in the sun. Maybe I will get a suntan. Then… I will spend sometime with your daughter, you both have developed a penchant for delivering decisions I did not see coming."

Pope Sophyra stood by the steps down to the reflecting lake, a mug of coffee in her hand, a servant standing a respectful distance away from a small breakfast table that had been set up for her. Her Papal robes glistened in the early morning sun.

"Have you decided what you will tell Phaedra?" Asked Elect-Si.

"Do you realize what you have done? I am a vampire without enzymes. No ability to kill me if I want to. No way to convert a human to my kind. I… I feel so empty?" She sighed and looked down at her coffee and brought the mug to her lips. She sipped.

"You tried to spit at Lady Challis. You tried to damage her in whatever way you could. You missed and killed one of our servants. He had been with us for centuries. We all knew him well. You had to pay." Elect-Si's tone was hard and brittle.

"Do you know what you will say to Phaedra? From now on you will have to use your wits and skills at planning, and lying. Manipulation."

"I will be disowned by my own kind." Said Pope Sophyra turning to Elect-Si.

"Don't you care about that?"

"You will only be disowned if you tell them, or try and spit and they find out you can't anymore. Just add it to your list of things you will have to lie about."

Pope Sophyra slowly turned and looked at the breakfast table and walked over to it and sat down. She pointed to what she wanted on her plate.

"My mother used to be sympathetic to me!" she exclaimed and banged her fists on the table, making her place setting rattle and vibrate.

"You have a biological grip on me tighter than she ever did. You should be sympathetic to how I am feeling, to my needs. You fucking bitch! You have turned me into a human."

Elect-Si studied the woman in front of her. Now, without her ability to create and deliver enzymes, venom, she was not much more than a human. Yes! That was true. Her own time as a human, before that fateful night when she was bitten by that evil vampire and then bitten again by Lady Challis. But her memories of being human wear from ages past, long dresses, horse-drawn carriages. A strict social hierarchy. Poverty, child slavery. Sailing ships. Everything since then she had been experienced as a Vampire.

Humans can be respected for what they achieve within the limited boundaries of their short lives. This, the thing in front of her would live many centuries longer than a human and had the potential to achieve so much more, and so much respect simply because of living that much longer opened so many possibilities. She could achieve as a born "human" could not.

Her attention turned to the palace, and her husband. His life span was measured in seconds, minutes, hours, days, weeks, months, years, and decades. Compared to her immortality, a decade was a mere grain of sand, no … less than a grain of sand, it was an atom that made a grain of sand.

For a moment Elect-Si's mind slipped into the world of time, and her role of gatekeeper. All around her the plane of existence stretched away from her, the darkness of the past, life which had been lived and ended was behind her. The future, also dark, unknown and undefined stretched in front of her. She looked to her left. Pope Sophyra stood nervously looking down at her feet, not up and ahead to the possibilities that existed in the future yet to be illuminated. Elect-Si saw that she was paralyzed by fear of what a small shuffling of her feet might bring. Somehow, Elect-Si had to encourage her, push her, cajole her to take a step into the future.

Her mind came back to the present and Sophyra, now eating.

"Human, you are not. You will live centuries longer than they do. You have so much potential. Leave behind the games you played as a child… How far can I spit? How much venom can I create? Can I hit my target? Can I spit against the wind? Spit against a cross wind?"

Sophyra stopped eating for a long moment as she thought about what Elect-Si had said, what she meant behind the words. Her utensils moved shakily in her hands.

"You are denying me my childhood…"

"No!" I am denying you relying on the past to create your future. You have to step forward. You cannot move backward and you cannot move sideways. Phaedra will be everywhere and nowhere if you allow her. She is your challenge; she is much more potent than your childhood games."

"Potent because you took away my ability to spit … to kill!"

"I took away the crutch you thought you had. Spitting never was what made you strong. It never made you Pope of the Eastern Church. You became pope by your cunning. Your plan within plans. You manipulated around my mother because her plan had become slow moving, without focus. Your plan was fast and agile. Phaedra is your enemy. You must out maneuver her everywhere she is and where she has yet to go. You must create your future and make her fear your mind, and, your ability."

Sophyra looked down at her plate and slowly started pushing food around as if it were chess pieces and she was designing her next gambit.

Elect-Si slowly moved towards the table and indicated a place setting should be set for her. Oddly … strangely … she felt she could not allow Pope Sophyra's last meal at the palace to be a solitary one. She picked her food and slowly sat down facing Sophyra.

For a moment she looked at the palace. She would have to spend a lot more time with Manuel, precious time, he had so much to teach her, and she had so much to learn.

He was at home, with their daughters, caring for them, loving them and letting them sleep on his chest. She remembered a time, shortly after they were married when she had found herself watching the rhythmic rise and fall of his chest as he snoozed on the day bed.

So simple, so necessary.

Her sensitive hearing allowed her to listen to his heart beat and the pressure of his blood moving through his arteries, and veins.

She needed to know so much more about her husband. About being human. Her tongue flipped idly across her fangs, perhaps a son, she could so that. She could determine the sex of a child at the moment of conception.

In her mind's eye, she could see the sperm pressing against the wall of her egg. She could sense the energy of the little swimmer. Was it male? All energy, urgency, and pressure, demanding to be let in … to fertilize. Could it be female? Was it gentler and more seductive in the way it pressed for entrance? Does it rub against the wall trying to find a weak spot to enter? Or maybe that rubbing was seduction?

She would talk to him first; they would decide together.

Amunet sat next to Elect-Si, enjoying the stream in which her feet were making small circles. Across the stream, her other guide looked on.

"The thing I regret most about not being in physical form is the small pleasures of doing things like putting my feet in a small stream." He started to look enviously at the two pairs of feet.

"I used to enjoy the simplicity of it. The water seems to remove all stress and worry in a way that swimming in the lake does not."

Amunet looked up, and studied the guide.

"I thought you had started to be part of this world. You could touch things and move them?"

"Yes, that is true. But holding a glass is not the same as the sensation from running water over my feet, in the way you are experiencing it, I do not have that. At least not yet."

He grinned slyly at Elect-Si.

"By being here, at the edge of what is past and future existence … in the NOW, you send a powerful message to all who would try and breach the boundary." He sighed.

" … and yet you are not fixed in the NOW. You have become more than just the Gatekeeper. You have become the watcher. You are a disrupter. There have been no more attempts at crossing from the past into the NOW, or the future."

Elect-Si looked around at the endless rolling grass lands and the few trees dotted here and there. The blue Sky.

"This is Mongolia, isn't it?"

"The endless grasslands and the endless blue sky. Yes. But it is also the Pampas of Argentina, it is the lush grazing of Afrika."

He slipped down to the opposite bank of the stream and gently put his feet into the stream and watched in rapture as they changed the flow of the water to make circles and eddies around them.

"Just a little. Just a little, I can feel the flow of the water and how restful it is starting to make me." He smiled across at Elect-Si.

"Small steps."

Elect-Si breathed in the smell of the grass, the smell of the wild flowers, and the sweetness of the cloudless sky. The warmth of the sun was relaxing and soothing.

Her eyes were opened by the sound of rustling in the long tall grass as it waved in the gentle breeze. At first, she was aware of a small figure watching intently from behind a patch of extra-long, thick grasses. After a few minutes, the figure started to emerge. As she watched, her cane slipped to her side and the handle into her hand. Emma sensed something that told her Elect-Si needed something to hold on to.

As the figured moved out into the grasses that were only shoulder high, Elect-Si could see dark matted hair, very unkempt and crudely cut. The face was elfin and dirty, a large dark smear of sweat and grease on the forehead. The features were thinner than they should be. The eyes were intense, they concentrated on Elect-Si, flicking from side to side to take in her guide on the same side of the stream, and Amunet sitting to Elect-Si's left.

The clothing was dirty, smeared with age, from never being taken off. Cuffs were worn and ragged, there were tears on the sleeves and the front of the velvet coat that had been crudely stitched closed. Underneath the coat she could see an attractive brocaded dress that was also as dirty and unkempt as the coat. The hem was down in some places and torn in others.

On the child's feet, boots. They looked too big for her but she walked with practised ease in them. Elect-Si guessed they were made for a boy, perhaps a year older and bigger than the girl now wearing them.

Elect-Si's eyes were now drawn to the yellow David's cross the badge of a Jew in Nazi Germany. It was stitched onto the left breast of the coat.

"Maybe a Jew, put their feet in the stream and wash them?" The voice was bright and clear, with a distinctive Eastern European sound.

Elect-Si's eyes were fixed on the yellow badge that meant discrimination, disregard, inhumanity, and eventual death.

"Maybe a Jew put their feet in the stream and wash them?" The question was repeated.

"Yes ... yes. Of course."

The girl looked to her side, to Elect-Si's guide who gestured encouragement to the girl to sit and use the stream.

Slowly the girl sat down at the edge of the stream. As she did, she unbuttoned her coat so that she had more freedom to pull off her boots. The dress underneath showed more evidence of not having been taken off for a long time. It was smeared and blackened in places where hands would have been rubbed to clean them of something.

Slowly she pulled off her boots and held on to them close to her body as she dipped her feet into the clear-flowing water. At first the girl just let her feet rest on the bottom without doing anything, then slowly, as she watched Elect-Si and Amunet gently swirling their feet in the water, she did the same and seemed to enjoy the greater agitation of the water over her feet. She stood up and lay the boots down on the grass and then sat on them. It freed up the hand that was holding them but she still had control of her precious boots.

She looked around her slowly and carefully, in all directions. Checking to see if there was anyone around who ment her harm. Then she leaned over and started to movers the water between her toes to clean them. From her coat pocket, she took out a piece of wood. Each end was bound with string. The girl grasped each end and pulled them apart. Inside a crude knife that Elect-Si realized had been made from the broken blade of a much larger knife. Slowly the girl started to trim her toe nails.

"It is a long time since I have been able to do this. It has been a long time since I have seen clear clean water like this stream." As she finished, she put away the knife. Making sure the pocked was closed. She looked up at Elect-Si.

"I have not bathed for months. I know I smell." She looked at each of them in turn. If I slip into the water...?"

The question was left hanging in the air as the girl slipped into the stream, holding her coat and dress up around her arm pits. She rubbed vigorously with her hands on her thighs, lower belly, and her buttocks.

Elect-Si could see that her body was thin and boney. Hip bones showed clearly and some of the ribs. Her spine showed its bones clearly. She breathed in as she thought of her own daughters, well fed, and growing fast.

Malnutrition would hold back this girl from fully growing and create openings for disease that would be debilitating and rob her of the strength she had. Elect-Si pressed her lips together. She wanted to say something, but she held back.

Finally, the girl took off the coat and dress and laid them on her boots and quickly, abruptly, dunked her entire body in the stream several times and rubbed vigorously on her face, shoulders and belly.

She clambered out picking up her dress and slipped it over her shoulders. It was then that Elect-Si realized the dress was not something the girl had found and exchanged for whatever she had been wearing. She had owned it, and it had fitted well when she was well fed, fit and healthy. It was a remnant from another age when she had been happy and carefree. Yes! Carefree. It had been a very pretty dress when it was new. There were still a few bows in different colours. Once bright and colourful they were now faded and shabby, dirt was ingrained into them. Under the armpits the tell-tale white stains of sweat showed, the dress was not exchanged for something lighter in the hottest weather. She picked up the coat and slipped it on. Then she turned to the boots and pulled them on.

She stared at Elect-Si.

"Thank you for letting a Jew clean themselves in such a clean stream." The voiced faded away, and there was silence for a couple of minutes.

"You are the Gatekeeper."

Elect-Si felt the words were a statement, but the tone of the girl's voice made them a question she felt she had to answer.

"Yes. I am the Gatekeeper."

The girl continued to stare at Elect-Si. She said nothing for several minutes. Then abruptly she spoke, "Let me in to the future. You must. I was nine, just a few days from now I will be raped and beaten to death by a Nazi." The words came out with a gentle tone but held a stinging venom laden meaning.

Elect-Si returned the girl's stare, the intensity of the demand in her eyes was matched by Elect-Si's resistance.

"You lived a terrible life, one that no child should live and your death was horrifying. But I cannot let you into the future in which you do not exist as who you were then."

The girl continued to stare at Elect-Si and realized her guide, and Amunet, were also watching and listening.

"What would you do … what would you say if you were to learn that your daughters would face the same horrors as I every day? My life went from dolls and kittens and puppies to fighting off the grasping hands of people trying to take food from me as I ran home. Watching old men die in the street as I walked by. Learning how to go through their clothes for valuables before anyone else. Waking up to find not my favourite kitten next to me on my bed but a big rat. Grasping and holding that rat down and killing it by smashing its head with a piece of iron. I slept, and then ate the vile creature." With surprising ease, she spat into the stream and challenged Elect-Si to look at her, not the spit as it meandered down, and away.

"No. I will not let you cross over." Elect-Si said firmly though her heart was breaking inside at the thought of the girl returning to her time to suffer the fate she had described.

"They said you are a black-hearted, evil bitch. You are worse than the Nazi's." The girl again gathered a ball of phlegm and spat it into the stream.

Elect-Si locked her stare on the girl and in a moment found herself in a ghetto. It was night time. The sky was black and clear. The stars were out, the moon was fading into its last phase. There were only a few street lamps, there were few people out. She looked down to her right hand, her cane was in her left hand.

The girl looked up at Elect-Si.

"It is midnight. The shouts and … yes, screams are of things being done that I never paid any attention to. With you here they sound so terrible. But this was life in the evening."

They walked for half a block before reaching a cross street. Up and down the street people shuffled from one doorway to the next, always stopping to look inside, to see if there were anything they could take advantage of.

To their left, a door banged open and a boy, about 12 came storming out into the street. He paused for a moment to decide which way to run and that gave his pursuer just enough time to catch him by the collar. The boy struggled violently in desperation to escape the pursuer's grip.

The pursuer, a Nazi officer raised a club and brought it down hard on the boy's legs, snapping one at the knee. The boy screamed as the leg buckled under him and took on a strange swinging motion of its own. His other foot lost its footing and the boy fell to the ground with the knee of the Nazi landing on his chest forcing all the air out of the boys" lungs. In the doorway, a mother cried and screamed as she begged for her son to be let go.

The Nazi dragged the screaming boy into the door way and hissed at the woman.

"Next time I come around; this one will not interrupt us.

"He raised his club high above his head and prepared to bring it down on the boy's skull.

"I would not do that," said Elect-Si. Her words were clear and precise, but feminine.

The Nazi paused for a moment at the strangeness of the words, they somehow sounded like an order, an instruction that he were not prepared to carry out. He brought the club down on the boy's skull and broke it open, killing him. Then he turned quickly to face Elect-Si.

"Aren't you the pretty one, where have you been hiding? I would have had you a hundred times by now if I had found you earlier. Are you a general's whore?"

"I am the gatekeeper." Replied Elect-Si in a matter-of-fact voice.

The sound of coarse laughter built up in his throat and broke open on the street.

"A beautiful cane, with gold and some sort of light in the handle. You must be a general's whore to have kept hold of that in this stinking ghetto. Give it to me and I will look after you."

The moon disappeared from the sky along with the stars. The street disappeared and, in a moment, everything was blackness. A void so black there appeared no ground, no up or down, nothing to the right or the left. In front of her, the Nazi officer. He no longer held his club.

All around him small circles started to appear they grew larger and became frames, each frame holding memories of events in his life. Small movies playing out a unique moment over and over again. Each was filled with scenes of brutality, hatred for life, and all living beings.

Machine guns blazing at women and children lined up naked in a field, falling backwards into a pit. A line of children being held down and clubbed to death. People set alight and left to run around as they burned to death for the entertainment of their executioners. People packed into a church and the church set ablaze to burn down and those inside of it.

"The blackness … so … so complete." Muttered the Nazi.

"This blackness is the blackness in me. You think of yourself as the blackest hearted person in the world. You have done many terrible things against life, against other living beings, but here, now is a blackness you cannot comprehend."

The Nazi tried to rush at Elect-Si, but as hard as he tried, he could not get any closer to her.

"What is this?" he raged.

"Why cannot I get to you…"

"There is a girl, in a velvet coat…"

"Yes. I will have her virginity tomorrow, and she will die immediately after … no one else in the barracks will have her, only me." He gestured with his right hand but found he had no club to swing.

"You like killing children, don't you," Said Elect-Si as she pointed to a couple of window frames showing moments when the officer had sought out children, and clubbed them to death.

"And you like breaking things … you like breaking bone."

Slowly the officer looked at the windows Elect-I point to and smiled.

"Yes … yes, I do. Kill them, kill them before they breed."

The officer screamed and fell to the black ground.

"My legs … my feet!" he moaned loudly, and started to run down his chin and he frothed at the mouth. He arched his back and bellowed a terrible scream as his arms gave way under him.

"My arms…"

"Yes, that is right. This is what broken bones feel like. Every bone in your legs, feet, in your hands and arms are now broken. Let's continue exploring my blackness."

"No! No! I beg you … the pain." He screamed, and his back arched in an attempt to release some of the pain coursing through his body.

"Did you ever listen to a child begging? Begging for the beating to stop … for their death not to come. Did you stop?"

"No… Why would I? They are less than human … especially the Jews, the Bolsheviks." Hissed the officer.

"Then you give me no reason to stop. Not that I would stop, no … I have no reason to stop." The officer twisted horribly as his pelvis and then each of the vertebrae in his spine, his ribs were cracked, and opened.

" … finally, there is only one thing left to break like an egg."

"No! Please. Let me live."

"Why?"

There was no answer.

"Why?" repeated Elect-Si.

"Because you have more children to kill? You enjoyed being on the Eastern Front. Being able to kill and destroy without anyone saying, you could not."

There was still no answer … a few stumbling words seared with pain.

"Those were the good times…"

The moon started to glow in the sky and the stars appeared. In the door way of the building, hidden by the stairs up to the apartments Elect-Si and the girl stood and looked at the crumpled body in its Nazi uniform.

"What did you do?" asked the girl.

"Did you take him to your dark place? The one that is darker than anyone can imagine?"

"Yes."

"Was he scarred?"

"Yes, very. He likes to break things … with a club… I taught him what it is like to have broken bones. I broke every bone in his body, even the smallest was not spared. His skull is shattered. He will die soon. He will not rape you tomorrow. He will not club you to death tomorrow."

Elect-Si looked down at the club lying not far from the Nazi's hand. She touched it with the golden tip of her cane. The club immediately burst into flames and in a moment, it was ash. The long swishing coat of someone hurrying past was enough to create a small breeze that blew away the ash.

Elect-Si looked down at the girl who slowly took her eyes off the dying Nazi.

"Thank you. You have given me hope. I may die later in the week. But I will not die tomorrow. Hope is all I asked for when I came to the stream. But you knew that?"

"Yes. But I could also not allow you to pass into the future. Your time is here, now, it is tomorrow, and the next day. You must live out your existence in the time that you are present."

The girl looked up at Elect-Si.

"As good or bad as those times maybe?"

"Yes. Your soul, your spirit will learn something, and carry it in your karma into the next existence."

The girl slowly nodded.

"Will I survive the ghetto?"

Elect-Si felt something new surge within her. Like a door opening that had been closed, hidden, and secret. She could see the life path of the girl. She could see the path crossed and abused by so many other paths, but this one always stayed true. Eventually, the path led to a bright, sunny, desert place with all manner of vegetables growing there fed by flowing clean water from a hard dug well. An oasis shaded by palm trees. Clean, white, new buildings and homes ... not houses. The sky, clear, and covered in sparkling stars. A middle-aged woman sitting with a community of friends around a fire talking, laughing, smiling, a guitar playing. An empty plate in front of her, no food wasted. The same eyes looking across at her, the same strong stare. Words mouthed in her direction. A glass set down and filled but no one sitting there. The woman pushing it towards Elect-Si, "Thank you... Thank you." A glass raised in a toast.

"Yes. You will endure… It will be hard. Many life paths will cross yours but stay true to yourself, and you will survive."

Elect-Si looked back at the dying Nazi.

"When you hear the words Israel and kibbutz. Pay attention. When you have the opportunity to go. Do not hesitate for a moment."

The girl slowly looked up and smiled at Elect-Si and reached out to hold her hand.

"Israel is in the Torah." She said with a tone in her voice that implied Elect-Si should know that.

"It will be a new country, one that does not exist today. Go to where it will be as fast as your feet can carry you and do not stop until you reach it. Be a part of its birth."

The girl turned slightly so she could hold Elect-Si's hand with both of hers.

"I will take my mother with me; she does not walk very well. I need her to kiss me good night before I start dreaming."

Elect-Si looked into that intense stare which seemed to be softening … just a little.

"I am sorry. I see only one path."

The grip in her hand grew stronger … "will you kiss me goodnight?" The eyes looked up at Elect-Si with open hope.

Elect-Si caught the pain in her heart. How could she say no, but she knew that is what she must say? How could she favour one child out of all the children that have lived? That will live?

"Yes." Elect-Si felt her heart lighten at what she had just said.

"Not every night, let's make it a surprise. You are strong enough to dream your dreams by yourself."

"Thank you… Thank you, gatekeeper."

"Elect-Si. My name is Elect-Si."

"Thank you… Thank you, Elect-Si."

Elect-Si looked down at her feet swishing in the stream. Across from her, her guide had gone. Her cane rolled in her hand. Amunet was standing close to her.

Amunet held out her hand and helped Elect-Si stand. She held Elect-Si's head and kissed her.

"It is not always easy… I know."

www.ingramcontent.com/pod-product-compliance
Lightning Source LLC
Chambersburg PA
CBHW070528260626
47161CB00004B/1657